# the art of avoiding your alpha

## WILDWOOD

## LOLA GLASS

Cover by Francesca Michelon

https://www.merrybookround.com/

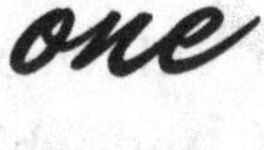

## TORI

I LIFTED the sugar cookie to my lips and took a small bite. The good things in life required savoring, after all. And while my cookie was good, work was eh, so I needed to savor my fifteen-minute break, too.

I was sitting down at a table in the front section of the bakery I worked at. My friends and I often ate there, because our break room was tiny.

My eyes moved over the other customers—most of them were regulars, so I recognized them—before catching on the single newcomer.

He was a man.

A beautiful man.

One with messy, dark hair, and light skin. Tattoos stretched over his gloriously-thick muscles, exposed by the simple black t-shirt he wore.

He was way too big to be human, and all the ink marked him visibly as some kind of shifter. Most of them had a ton of tattoos.

I wasn't really sure why they did, but I thought it was cool, so I supported the ink obsession.

Considering we lived in Wildwood, I'd put money on the hottie being a werewolf. And while I didn't think I'd ever seen him before, the pack was growing rapidly, so that wasn't entirely surprising.

His attention was fixed on the laptop in front of him, and there was a crease between his eyebrows. He obviously hadn't noticed me.

"Who is that?" I asked Sienna, one of my two best friends. She was average height, wearing a pair of comfortable-looking black leggings and an oversized sweatshirt with a cat on it. She'd been unhealthily thin when she first got to Wildwood, but her curves had filled out gorgeously in the months since.

Her gaze was on the view outside *Coffee & Toffee & Cake*'s front windows. We worked in the *Cake* portion, but enjoyed the smells of both coffee and baked goods all day long.

She glanced over at the guy... and stared for a long moment.

"No idea," she finally said, looking back out the window.

Unlike hers, my attention didn't move.

She sipped her coffee, and I took another bite of my cookie.

"Stop staring at him," Sienna murmured, after a few minutes had passed. "Someone's going to take a picture of you staring and post it online or something."

She and I, along with our other friend Lovene, were blood wolves. Vampire/werewolf hybrids.

Love had mated to the alpha of the Wildwood pack, the biggest wolf pack in the world, six months earlier. Her mate Archer Madden (AKA Madd), was well-known. His connections in the government dealt with the cruel vampire clan who had made my friends and I what we were.

So, we were free.

And members of the pack.

But, blood wolves were basically known for being used by vampires as living blood bags. It made us constant targets.

We were safe in Wildwood.

But, being the only blood wolves in town meant there were obnoxious humans with social media pages dedicated to watching our every move.

I was still adjusting to that.

Anyway, we were figuring it out.

And the pack was kind to us, which is what really mattered.

Love sat down in the seat beside mine, and my head snapped toward her.

Hadn't even noticed her crossing the room.

Whoops.

She had on her typical fishnets, high-tops, and t-shirt dress with the logo of some band none of us had ever heard of, including her. Her hair was a pretty, medium-brown shade, with waves cropped to her chin and bangs that fell artfully over her forehead. She was short with some curves, and her skin was light, but tanned thanks to the sun.

"Who are you staring at?" she asked me.

"A sexy new werewolf guy," I said.

She snorted, looking around the room. "There are three werewolf guys in here. None of them are new."

"The dark-haired dude directly across from her," Sienna said.

"Oh, Vex? You haven't met him?"

"That would be a no." I didn't look away from him.

I wasn't sure I could if I tried.

"He's the guy in the Supernatural Government who saved Sienna from the clan. Technically, he's an alpha, too. Madd gave him and his pack a chunk of land at the edge of the city. They're staying here for a while to make a statement that the wolves aren't going to let any vampires use us."

That news probably should've made me look away.

It didn't.

"Does he smell good to you?" Love asked, studying me.

I lifted an eyebrow at her. "Seriously? He's not my mate."

A wolf shifter could only identify their potential mate through scent. If he smelled really great, that would be a sign that I needed to get the hell out before he realized what I was to him. A male werewolf would never walk away from his fated mate.

Luckily, all I could really smell was coffee and cupcakes.

Just the most attractive man I'd ever seen.

"I was just asking. And having a fated mate isn't the end of the world." She bumped my arm with her elbow.

"Agree to disagree." I took another bite of my cookie, brushing crumbs off my bright pink sports bra. Despite the cold outside given that it was the beginning of February in our forest-town, all I was wearing was that and a pair of high-waisted leggings, like usual. Thick clothes bothered me. I liked being able to move.

I was tall, slim, and pale, with my strawberry-blonde hair cut in a pixie that was long enough on the top to fall to my cheekbones. I hoped the spunk of it would somehow scare off any men looking for real relationships.

"I'm with her on this one. Not at all interested in taking a mate," Sienna agreed.

"You'd change your mind if you knew what it's like," Love countered.

My next bite of my cookie was bigger.

And a bit more violent.

I had *zero* interest in pairing up permanently with anyone. Particularly an alpha. The last thing I wanted was someone giving me orders. I'd slept with a few of the human men in the city since I moved in, just to get some experience so no one could catch me off-guard.

I forced my attention to the windows I was supposed to be looking at.

Wildwood was a beautiful city, with the buildings nestled in the forest so everything felt tucked away. It wasn't anywhere near small, but still felt like it was.

"Is he looking at her now?" Sienna whispered, and my head jerked back to the side.

My gaze collided with Vex's for a moment, and I froze.

I waited for him to look away...

But he didn't.

And I couldn't take my eyes off him.

*"He's so pretty,"* my wolf murmured into my mind. When one of us wasn't in control, we were tucked away in some sort of in-between, the way she currently was. We could always communicate, though my wolf was pretty damn laid-back compared to what I'd heard of Love's.

*"Tall, buff, and scary,"* I protested, though I didn't believe it.

*"We like tall, buff, and scary."*

She was right.

We really, really did.

Vex's nostrils flared before he finally dragged his gaze away from mine, looking back down at his computer.

I forced my eyes to the window again.

"That was hot," Love remarked. "Are you sure he doesn't smell good to you? I know your scent is hidden with perfume."

I wore an assload of perfume, actually.

And scented lotion.

*Everywhere.*

I wasn't about to get accidentally paired with someone.

Not even someone as gorgeous as Vex.

"If she wants a whiff, she'll go over and talk to him," Sienna said.

I didn't want a whiff.

Well, I did, but I wasn't willing to risk getting mated.

So, I stayed put.

They chatted as I made myself keep staring out the window, but I tuned out their voices.

Because I couldn't stop my mind from going back to the way my abdomen had tightened when he looked at me.

A few moments passed before I caught a smell.

A *delicious* smell.

And felt a tap on my shoulder.

When I turned my head, I found Vex standing right next to my table.

I couldn't stop my eyes from widening.

I couldn't stop myself from taking in a deep lungful of his scent.

Or my fangs from descending.

Fuck, I wanted to taste him.

"Hello," he said smoothly.

"Um," I said, words suddenly failing me.

Holy shit, he smelled incredible.

"Hi," I managed, trying to talk around my fangs without cutting myself.

My friends had gone silent, and neither of them were intervening in the conversation for my sake.

That wasn't good.

"I'm Ronin." He held out a hand. "I assume you're one of the blood wolves, given your company." Despite knowing Love, he didn't so much as glance her way.

That was a bad sign.

Very bad, considering I didn't want a mate.

"Yep. Tori." I awkwardly shook his hand, and my fangs descended further.

The damn things needed to chill out.

"Can I buy you coffee?" he asked.

I glanced at the line.

There was no line, so there was no real excuse.

But I needed to get away from him so I could breathe again.

And so I didn't bite the guy.

"I'm not thirsty," I finally said, cutting my tongue a bit deeper with that one.

"Another cookie, then." He plucked the small remains of my cookie away from me, popped them in his mouth, then took my hand and towed me to my feet.

I shot my friends a look that screamed "HELP" as Ronin led me across the bakery.

Love was grinning madly.

Sienna's expression was worried.

His hand found the small of my back as he ordered, and it felt way too good.

I stared at the display case full of the heart and arrow cookies Sienna had decorated for Valentine's Day, which was only two days away.

My heart pounded madly.

His smell surrounded me, and shit, it was heavenly.

My fangs sank further into my lip, making me wince while Elizabeth packed our cookies into a to-go box.

He studied me. "Are you okay?"

"I'm fine," I said.

The movement must've flashed my bleeding lip at him somehow, because his frown deepened as he caught my chin.

I went still.

My lips parted with a bit of gentle pressure, revealing my fangs.

He dragged his thumb lightly over my cut, then released me.

And lifted his thumb to his nose, and inhaled.

I shuddered as he caught my scent, his chest rumbling and his eyes gleaming. "I knew it."

*"This isn't good,"* my wolf murmured.

*"Not in the slightest,"* I whispered back.

"Hmm?" I feigned confusion.

His thumb slid between my lips again, and slowly dragged over my descended fang.

The touch was light enough that I couldn't draw blood without biting down—and my body trembled as I fought the urge to do so.

My fangs were sensitive. *Insanely* sensitive.

It felt like he had a finger on my nipple, or between my thighs.

He pulled his hand away again, but my body continued trembling. Every sense I possessed screamed at me to move closer.

To wrap my arms around him.

To sink my teeth into his skin and drink until I was gloriously sated.

"You're mine, Tori." His voice was low and smooth.

Just as hot as the rest of him.

Dammit, I was in trouble.

I lied anyway. "I have no idea what you're talking about."

My words were steady. Steadier than the rest of me, at least.

"Bite me, then." His gaze was wicked.

Wicked, and determined.

"Excuse me?" I raised my voice.

"If you're not my mate, prove it. You can feed on me without growing addicted. Bite me."

"We're in a public place—and my workplace, at that," I hissed back, regaining a bit of my composure now that he wasn't stroking my fangs. "And I don't have to prove anything."

Rather than arguing with me, he grabbed me by the hips.

And threw me over his shoulder.

My yelp accompanied my face, as it smashed against Vex's back.

*Ronin* Vex's back.

He grabbed the box of cookies, turned on his heels, and strode out the door.

# two

## RONIN

I'D FINALLY FOUND my mate, after she'd hidden herself from me with *perfume*.

Now, I wasn't letting her go until I was confident she wasn't going to run.

The woman was going to be mine, and she was going to fucking love it.

My fingers clenched on the steering wheel as the scent of her perfume filled my truck's cab.

I needed to smell her.

To touch her.

To talk to her.

But she had hidden herself from me and pretended not to know she was mine, so I couldn't risk saying anything until she was in my house, where I was in control.

My phone started ringing.

Madd's name was on the caller ID.

I stabbed the button to answer it. "What?"

There was a beat of silence before he spoke. "I think you can guess why I'm calling."

There had been people at the bakery.

Humans.

His mate, too.

All of them had seen me throw my female over my shoulder, claiming her.

*Good.*

"She's mine. I'm not letting her go until she's accepted it," I said.

*"Caution may be important here,"* my wolf grumbled.

*"Fuck caution."*

"Tori is one of my mate's best friends," Madd said, his voice even. "You can't just abduct her from the middle of the damn bakery."

"I don't care who she is to your mate; she's mine."

"You know I'm going to have to send my enforcers after her. This sets a dangerous precedent. If I don't punish someone for taking one of our blood wolves, my mate could be next."

"I didn't take a blood wolf, I took my mate. Send your people after me—I'll kill whoever I have to, to keep her. My pack will too."

"This escalated way too quickly," Tori said, shooting me a look.

I didn't see whatever emotion was in her eyes, because I had to watch the road.

"Are you okay?" Love demanded, her voice replacing Madd's.

"I'm fine. He can't hurt me, right?"

I growled at the question, and my wolf did too.

"No, he can't hurt you," Love said quickly.

"Then we'll get this sorted out, and I'll be back home tonight. Don't send anyone after us."

Love paused for a moment before she finally said, "Alright. Take care of yourself."

"I always do. I'll see you soon."

"You'd better!"

Tori hit the button to end the call as I turned down the first dirt road that led toward my house.

The few houses on the outer chunk of the city Madd had given my pack were rundown, so we'd all started working on them as soon as we moved in. Given the presence of the blood wolves, I assumed we'd need to stay close for a long, long time.

The foundation to my place was solid and the floorplan was decent, so the work hadn't been too bad.

It kept me busy, which was what mattered.

"Where are we going?" Tori asked me.

"My house."

She didn't shrink away from me at the admission, which seemed like a good sign.

I turned onto another dirt road.

My nostrils flared as the scent of her perfume hit me again.

The woman was going to drive me insane.

*"Breathe,"* my wolf rumbled. *"We need her to like us."*

*"We can worry about that after she's in our house, clean, and smelling right."*

He huffed at me, but didn't protest further.

"How far away from the pack's neighborhood do you live?" Tori asked me, after a few minutes of tense silence as I continued flying through the forest.

"Thirty minutes on the roads. Fifteen through the trees." I had to grit the words out.

More time passed, until I finally stopped in front of my home. It was expansive, with large windows I'd had to replace, and rotted siding I'd had to tear out and redo. The dark green paint still looked fresh, and the wraparound porch—though it needed more work—made the place look welcoming.

Tori was still looking at the house when I plucked her out of the passenger seat and carried her inside.

I still wasn't thinking straight.

Wasn't sure I ever would again, honestly.

"I have legs," she grumbled, when I carried her over the threshold and straight into the one functional bathroom I had. It was in the hallway. The master was going to take longer to fix, so I'd started with the hall one.

Holding Tori to my chest, I turned the water on. I knew better than to toss my mate below the falling water without making sure it was warm, so I gave it a minute to heat.

"If you try to strip me down, I will figure out how to kill you," she warned me. "Mate bond be damned."

"At least you admit there's a mate bond."

She huffed, but said nothing else.

I tested the water.

It was warm enough, so I set her down on her feet beneath it.

Her perfume's scent finally died down, and my shoulders relaxed as she glared at me from where she stood beneath the water.

"You really thought throwing a woman in a shower was necessary, Ronin?"

"You really thought hiding your scent from an alpha was necessary, Tori?"

"Madd's my alpha." She pushed a few loose, wet strands of hair off her face.

"Not anymore."

She huffed and peeled her electric blue leggings down her thighs, revealing a thong that was a slightly lighter shade of blue.

My cock hardened as she stepped out of the drenched pants, my eyes moving slowly down her figure.

The woman was stunning.

Lithe body.

Bright pink sports bra holding her perfect breasts.

Fuck, I wanted to pull it down and put my mouth on them.

Tori tossed her pants on the rug. "If I wanted a mate, I would've come over to talk to you."

"If you hadn't been hiding your scent, I would've claimed you the moment you walked into that bakery."

"I'm not an object you can just claim!" She pushed hair out of her eyes, and it took everything I had not to grab her and kiss her. "Or someone you can just throw in the shower. What the hell is that about?"

"You smelled like perfume. I fixed that."

"There was nothing to *fix*. That was intentional. Now I'm soaked, and you're just staring at me, dry as a fucking bone." She tossed her hand toward me, as if making a point. "This whole situation is—what are you doing?"

She cut herself off when I stepped into the shower, my chest colliding with hers.

She didn't step back.

I hoped she wouldn't.

My hands lifted to her waist.

I couldn't stop them any more than I could make my erection go down.

She took in a slow breath, and her body arched against mine just slightly. "You smell too good."

"You look fucking delicious."

She arched a bit more. "You're hard."

"Ridiculously so."

The defense in her eyes eased slightly. "Can you smell me yet?"

I tilted my head down, dragging my nose over the sensitive skin on the side of her neck before I inhaled.

My fingers dug into her waist.

My cock throbbed against her abdomen.

She was perfect.

"Mate." My wolf's growl rolled through the room.

Tori's body pressed tighter to mine, trembling slightly. "Are you sure?"

"Fucking positive." My hands slid up her back, and she leaned closer.

Her breasts pressed against me, and my gaze followed a trail of water between them.

She still smelled like that damn perfume.

I forced my hand off her hip long enough to grab a pump of soap, then rubbed it over her neck. She jumped a bit at the contact, but tilted her head to the side when she realized what I was doing.

"You're still wearing clothes," she told me, finally lifting her hands to rest on my chest.

Her touch felt incredible.

"If I strip, you're going to end up pinned to that wall with my cock buried inside you."

"Is that supposed to dissuade me?"

My chest rumbled again, and I fought the urge to let my hands slide down to her ass.

"In all seriousness, we're not having sex until we decide what's happening between us," she said.

"That's pretty damn simple. We seal the bond. You move in with me. Happily ever after."

She rolled her eyes. "That's cute."

I frowned.

She took a step back, and I reluctantly let her put a little space between us.

"I'm not sealing a bond with someone I don't know. I'm definitely not *moving in* with someone I don't know. I've been through way too much shit to risk myself that way."

My frown deepened.

I knew the process of making a blood wolf.

My female had been through more hell than anyone should ever experience. I couldn't push her into anything as far as our relationship went.

"Tell me what you're comfortable with, then."

"Going home and pretending this never happened."

I scowled. "No."

"Then this whole situation is outside my comfort zone." Her eyes lingered on my face for a minute before they slowly moved down my body. "On second thought, maybe you *should* strip."

"We're not having sex until I know what's happening between us," I grumbled.

Her lips curved upward.

"What would make you more comfortable right now, other than leaving?" I asked.

"Getting out of this shower and drying off, I'd say. And finding something to eat. I'm hungry."

"Alright. Get all the perfume off your skin, and I'll cook."

"Yes, Alpha," she drawled.

When she shooed me, I reluctantly stepped out of the shower.

My gaze ran over her figure again.

The view was so damn good, I could live with the space between us.

For the moment, at least.

# three

## TORI

RONIN STAYED EXACTLY where he was, watching me as I scrubbed myself with his soap. It smelled masculine, which I wasn't used to. I usually went to town with the fruity or floral stuff, and always smelled strongly like it.

The shower, like the rest of the house that I'd seen (minus the iffy porch), looked brand new.

And fancy.

The tile was shiny and perfect.

The walk-in shower was luxurious.

Everything was spacious and comfortable.

I liked it more than I wanted to.

Since he didn't leave, I didn't strip out of my underwear. They didn't cover a whole lot of me, but enough to give me some amount of privacy and therefore security.

When I stepped out, he had a towel waiting for me.

It was bizarre.

Insanely bizarre.

I'd never had someone wrap a towel around me before.

Or brush the random loose, wet strands off the back of my neck.

"You don't have to do that," I said.

"I get to do whatever I want with you, Tor." His hands landed on my shoulders, and I bit back a groan when he massaged them lightly. "Assuming you're on board with it, of course. I'll get you one of my shirts to wear."

"Put on some dry clothes while you're at it."

He chuckled. "Yes ma'am."

Was that a hint of a southern accent?

He was way too attractive for my good.

Ronin finally let go and stepped out of the bathroom. He left the door open, but I closed it behind him.

Leaning up against the thick wood, I squeezed my eyes shut and tried to process everything that had just happened.

Staring at him in the coffee shop.

Getting thrown in his truck, then set in the shower.
Watching him eye-fuck me.

Feeling his body against mine, with his attraction to me very, very evident.

Shaking my head, I stripped out of my underwear and rewrapped the towel around me.

Ronin turned the doorknob, and I stepped away just as he opened it. Instead of coming inside, he just looked into the bathroom.

His eyes heated again when he saw me, despite the towel I still wore. "Damn, woman."

My face warmed, just slightly. Not enough for him to notice how much I appreciated the compliment, I hoped.

When I held my hand out, he put a bundle of clothes in it. "I'll start lunch."

I nodded, and he took one last look at me before he stepped back, leaving the door open.

I closed it.

And locked it, for good measure.

PULLING his t-shirt over my head made me feel... uncertain.

Really uncertain.

I studied myself in the mirror for a long moment.

Same slight curves.

Same blue eyes.

Same strawberry-blonde hair, though my curls were soaked and straight.

The gray t-shirt Ronin had loaned me fell to the tops of my thighs, and did little to hide the points of my nipples.

Oh well.

After letting out a long, slow breath, I gathered my clothes and slipped out of the bathroom. "Where's your dryer?" I called out, peering down both sides of the hallway.

"Third door on the left," Ronin called back.

I walked down that way, and stepped into the door that would be third on the left if I was coming from the main living area. Just inside, I halted.

The room was... off.

The tile in it matched the rest of the house, brand new and beautiful, but the walls were a terrible shade of tan. There were a few holes in them, as well as a ton of dirt and some suspicious-colored stains. The window looked brand new, but the ceiling was popcorn-style, and the whole room smelled weird.

Eyeing a large hole in the wall, I put my clothes in the dryer, tossing in a few fresh-smelling sheets I found on top of it.

I figured there was probably, *hopefully*, a logical explanation for the odd laundry room, so I padded back down the hall-way. I'd seen a large, open kitchen and living area when Ronin carried me to the bathroom, so I headed that way.

I found him without a problem.

He was wearing nothing but a pair of sweats, and standing with his back to me. Something sizzled on the stove, and he inhaled deeply.

As soon as my scent hit him, he was looking over his shoulder.

His gaze was hot on my figure.

Instead of going over to him, I sat down at a chair. His kitchen table was gorgeous, and large enough that eight chairs fit around it comfortably.

"Your food's going to burn," I remarked, when he was still staring at me a minute later.

His attention jerked back to the stove, and I let my eyes move down his back.

Hot damn, the view was great in his kitchen.

Especially because he was shirtless.

And the way those sweats clung to has backside?

Yumm.

I peeled my eyes away from him a few minutes later, when he started putting the plates together. Forcing my gaze to the windows, I made myself look at the forest.

That view was good too.

I padded across the kitchen and into the living room, pulling the door open. A wave of icy air washed over me, and I took a deep breath in.

I couldn't see or hear the city, or anyone from the pack.

It was silent.

Peaceful.

Calm.

I could get used to that kind of privacy.

"Food's ready," Ronin rumbled, and I heard him pull a chair out.

I closed the door and walked back. My gaze lingered on his bare abdomen when I found him standing at the table, holding a chair out for me.

Shit, he was pretty.

I took the seat he'd offered me, remaining quiet until he sat down too. His food was across the table from mine.

"Eggs, bacon, and hashbrowns?" I lifted an eyebrow when he sat down across from me.

"I don't cook often, so I don't have much for ingredients," he admitted.

"You buy takeout for every meal?" I cut into the eggs. They were a perfect medium—slightly runny, but not liquid. My favorite.

"Probably half the time. I eat with my pack the other half. Cooking isn't an enjoyable chore when there's no one to share the meal with."

I could understand that.

I hadn't liked cooking much until Sienna moved in with me. After she did, I started making most of our meals, and I actually had fun with it. I had a whole list of recipes to try on my phone, and I just picked a few out when I was planning what to make for the next week. We were constantly trying new things, and it was fun.

We ate in silence, though there was quiet music playing in the background that made the situation feel more comfortable. I was pretty sure it was rock music, though it wasn't loud enough for me to hear the words or really figure it out.

When we finished, he leaned back in his chair and studied me.

I leaned back in mine, letting my gaze move down him again.

Ronin really *was* gorgeous.

"So, what are we going to do?" he asked me.

"I don't know," I admitted. "I don't want a mate."

"And I've been searching for mine for nearly two centuries."

I grimaced.

His gaze lingered on my face.

"I need time to think about it," I finally said. "Time to talk to my friends. To work through it in my mind. To figure out what I'm willing and not willing to do."

"I'm not letting you go without some guarantee that you won't walk away for good." He was calm, but there was no question in his tone.

He wasn't letting me leave without something bonding us.

As much as his words frustrated me, I grudgingly respected him for not letting me make all of the rules.

He was right; I would start trying to figure out how to get away if he gave me the chance.

"What do you suggest?" I asked.

His gaze remained fixed on me. "Seal the bond, move in with me, or drink my blood."

I blinked.

Sealing the bond would make my wolf unwilling to leave his. If I left Wildwood, she'd take over and run right back.

Leaving Wildwood wasn't even a real option, though. Blood wolves were rare, and valuable to vampires. If I left, there would be no one to protect me, and there was a damn good chance some vampire or another would find me.

There wasn't a chance in hell I'd ever subject myself to that willingly again.

So, leaving was out of the question.

Even if we lived separately, sealing the bond would make everything between us permanent. My wolf would probably run back to him whenever she got the chance, and I shifted every day or two, so it would be often.

Drinking his blood wouldn't be quite as bad as sealing the bond. I'd still be tied to him permanently, because drinking a potential mate's blood made you completely addicted to them. All other blood would taste foul, if not downright sickening.

But I only needed to feed once a week. If I shifted at all, then twice.

Moving in together would be worse than sealing the bond or drinking his blood. It wasn't as permanent, but Ronin would have an intimate view into my life. I would have no way to get away from him, because my home would be his.

That was out of the question.

So, my options were to seal the bond or drink his blood.

Of the two choices, drinking his blood would give me more space from him. And more space meant more freedom, which I was completely and entirely on board with.

On top of the space, if I really wanted to, I could probably stop drinking his blood and still survive. It would lead to a very hellish decade, but I'd already survived one hellish decade when the clan had me. What was one more?

There was absolutely no escape from a sealed mate bond. That shit was permanent, for the rest of our lives and what-ever came after.

So, the best option was clear.

"I'll drink your blood," I said.

Satisfaction flared in his eyes. "Alright. After you drink from me, I'll take you home and give you a few hours to process everything."

"A few hours? That's nowhere near enough time, *Alpha*," I fired back.

"What do you suggest?"

"A few weeks."

He scoffed. "I'd lose my mind trying to stay away from you for that long. Not happening."

"One week, then."

His scowl deepened. "No."

"Five days, at least."

"*One* day."

"Four."

"One-and-a-half."

"Three."

"Two."

I shot him an exasperated look. "Seriously, Ronin?"

"Two days is a lot." His gaze was hard.

"Fine, I'll make two work."

"You give me your phone number, and answer whenever I text you," he added. "I'll need to know you're okay frequently."

My exasperation grew.

"Staying away from you is going to cause me physical pain, Tor. You get two days of freedom in exchange for answering my texts. If you don't answer, you get my wolf at your door, following you around through both days."

His wolf?

That was more manageable than him, at least.

And I liked the way he'd shortened my name. It had sass.

"I don't want to cause you pain," I said, combing my fingers through my damp hair. "What if you give me the afternoon and evening alone, and when I text you tonight, you let your wolf come to me? You could stay in that form for a few more days, to give me more time."

The intensity in his gaze eased slightly. "That would work."

I let out a relieved breath. "At least that's settled."

"It will be, after my blood is in your veins."

Right.

I'd purposefully forgotten about that bit.

I combed my hair with my fingers again. "What if we let go of the blood thing, and I just let your wolf keep me company for a while?"

"Not happening."

I sighed.

Ronin still didn't budge.

"Fine, I'll drink your blood." I paused, scrambling to come up with another way out of binding myself to him. I had nothing. "When I'm ready."

"Take your time." He stood, grabbing our empty plates.

My gaze followed him to the sink—and a bit of guilt set in as I watched him run the water.

He'd already cooked for me.

I couldn't leave him to do the dishes himself, even if he had just whisked me away from work and thrown me in his shower.

On second thought, that *did* seem like a good enough reason to make him do the cleaning.

But, my guilt wouldn't allow it.

"I'll clean up," I said, standing and crossing the room. But when I stepped up beside him, he didn't move.

"I've got it."

I reached over and plucked the sponge from his hand. The plate, too.

He stole them back immediately.

When I tried to take them again, he lifted them up high. I was tall for a woman, coming in around 5'11", but he was at least six-and-a-half feet.

Which meant his arms were much longer than mine.

"You cooked, so I need to clean," I argued.

"You don't need to do anything except sit at the table and look like my fucking gorgeous mate."

I couldn't help the goosebumps that broke out over my arms. "That's not how this is going to go, Ronin."

"Last I heard, you hadn't decided how it was going to go."

He was right.

I hadn't.

But I did know I wasn't jumping into a mate bond where we weren't equals.

"If one of us cooks, the other cleans up. That's how it's going to work," I shot back, going up on my tiptoes to try to reach the sponge.

He lifted it higher.

I growled, turning and stepping between him and the sink. My chest met his, the thin fabric of my borrowed t-shirt the only thing between my chest and his.

The hem of the shirt barely covered my lower half.

He stepped closer, and his erection met my pelvis.

My body warmed.

"Just give me the sponge," I said, my voice a little strained.

"Just accept that I'm doing the damn dishes." His voice was low, and smooth.

More goosebumps spread over my arms.

My hands lowered to his shoulders.

He finally moved the sponge back down.

I spun and ripped it out of his grasp.

The plate, too.

He was hard against my lower back as his hands reluctantly landed on my hips, and he gave me a low, sexy chuckle.

More goosebumps followed.

His smell... it was in my lungs, despite the soap's scent mingling with it in the air.

"You're stubborn, Tor."

"So are you, Alpha." I ignored the way my heart beat rapidly in my chest, and forced myself to remain calm as I scrubbed the dish.

He ran his fingers lightly over my hipbones. The touch was much more intimate than any of the sloppy, drunken sex I'd had with human men.

That had been an attempt to prove to myself that the clan didn't control me anymore. All it had done was made me feel more out of control, and less certain of everything.

Yet when Ronin touched me, it was different.

It made me warmer, and wetter.

His erection remained between us, unspoken evidence of the bond he wanted.

"You shouldn't touch me until I've decided what I'm comfortable with," I said, my voice strained as I continued washing the dishes.

"You shouldn't take the dishes from my hands if you don't want me to touch you." He squeezed lightly.

I fought like hell to ignore the way I was starting to want him. "You don't get to both cook and clean up for me. You're not here to serve me."

"I'd be happy to serve you in every way there is, Tor." His hands slid slowly down from my hips, and I clenched my thighs tightly.

I was unaffected by him.

Completely unaffected by him.

Maybe if I kept repeating that to myself, it would somehow become true.

His lips brushed my ear as he leaned in a bit harder. "With my hands. My mouth. My tongue. My cock."

My legs started trembling a little.

Just a little.

"You forgot your mind," I said.

His lips brushed my ear as they moved, and I couldn't suppress a shiver. "It's focused on you too." His hands moved back up to my hips, squeezed again, and remained. "I'll wait until you're ready."

"I'll never be ready." The words slipped out before I could consider them.

His tongue dragged slowly over the three piercings in my earlobe. "I'll get you ready."

Finally, he released my hips and took a step back.

He didn't go far, though.

From the corner of my eye, I watched him cross the kitchen lazily, then sit down at the table again.

His gaze never left me.

"Your laundry room was interesting," I said, trying to force the conversation into safer territory.

"I've been renovating the place since I moved in. Haven't gotten to the laundry room yet."

Ah.

Dammit, there *was* a reasonable explanation.

And he was clearly good at what he was doing, because the house looked incredible.

"You're not busy with your work for the Supernatural Government?"

"No. There's some paperwork, but otherwise there's not much to it. They reach out when they need me, I spend a few days helping, and there's radio silence until they need me again. Usually, it's only a few times a year. Most supernaturals are old enough and smart enough to deal with their own shit as much as possible."

That checked out, though I'd add *sneaky enough to hide as much of their own shit as possible.*

The vampires who'd created me and my friends had kept us a secret for far too long.

"And you've done all the work yourself?" I gestured to the kitchen.

"For the most part. Swapped labor with a few guys in the pack who're better with plumbing and electrical."

Hot damn.

The cabinets were gray, the tiled backsplash was white, and the countertops were stone. It was honestly beautiful. Between that and the new flooring, the fresh paint on the walls, and the gorgeous bathroom... the man was clearly good.

Except at plumbing and electrical.

But hey, he had to have *some* imperfections.

Outside the abducting-me-from-my-workplace bit.

"That's amazing," I said honestly.

"It's good to stay busy." His voice was... uncomfortable.

He didn't seem to know what to do with the compliment.

When I peeked over at him, I found his face a bit red.

That was kind of adorable.

I didn't say anything about it, of course. What alpha werewolf wanted to be called adorable?

Probably not the one watching me wash dishes like it was his personal show.

Not a very sexy show, but hey, to each their own.

"How much of the house do you have left?"

"Not too much." He gave me a quick rundown of everything. It might not have been much to him, but it sounded like a lot to me.

He finished up his list as I put the last of our dishes in the dishwasher. Including the pan, because life was too short to hand-wash anything.

When I looked over my shoulder to see if he'd have a problem with the pan going in the dishwasher, he was still watching me intently.

I could definitely get used to that kind of attention.

But, I couldn't let myself. Not if I wanted to retain my freedom.

So, I closed the dishwasher.

If I wanted to get away from him to get that thinking time I'd bargained for, I was going to have to drink his blood.

Sooner, rather than later.

And well, there was no time like the present. Might as well get that difficult shit over with.

So, I crossed the room, trying not to let my nerves show.

Ronin didn't say a word as I walked toward him.

Or as I sat down on his lap, straddling him.

I barely suppressed a sharp inhale when his hands landed low on my hips, right above my ass.

"Have you ever fed a vampire before?" I asked him, my voice shaking slightly.

"No. The idea is pretty simple, though."

"The venom isn't. It affects everyone to different degrees. Some people can control themselves for the most part—others are lost to the venom."

"You're worried I'll lose control?" His gaze was hot, but not angry or irritated.

He honestly wanted to know.

"No, I'm not worried. Even if you do, the worst that could happen is us having sex. Which wouldn't exactly be a hardship." After a beat, I added, "Pun not intended."

"I don't lose control, Tor."

"Okay, *Alpha*, but this is me warning you. Everyone's affected differently. Even if the impact isn't too strong, you'll be so horny, you won't be able to think straight."

"I'm already horny enough that I can't think straight. Bite me."

He squeezed my hips, and I sucked in another breath.

My fangs descended of their own volition.

It wasn't really my fault if he wasn't willing to listen to me... so I leaned forward.

And I bit him.

It was the end of my freedom. I knew it was—I was going to be addicted to him afterward.

But he wasn't letting me out of his house if I didn't, so it was the better choice.

And despite it being the end of my freedom, I couldn't help my soft gasp at the taste of him.

He was... everything.

Sweet, and sour.

Tangy and fresh.

Calm, and powerful.

Holy shit, he tasted *incredible*.

His chest rumbled. I barely noticed it, I was so lost in the taste of him.

Everything that happened next felt as if it was in a haze.

He dragged me across his lap, so my chest met his.

Once again, the thin fabric of his shirt was the only thing between us.

My nipples were hard and pointed.

His hands slid down—and found my ass.

My *bare* ass.

His chest rumbled more fiercely, and he squeezed.

My body arched of its own volition, pressing harder against him.

The haze faded, and was replaced immediately by need.

Thick, wild, *intense* need.

I took a deep pull of his blood, flooding my senses.

One of his hands slid roughly up my torso, finding my breasts. His thumb dragged over the point—and I moaned against his shoulder, taking more of his blood.

My hands found the button of his jeans between us, and made quick work of the metal. I had his cock free in a heart-beat, and dragged my hands up the hard, silky length of him.

He snarled, his hand on my breast tightening almost painfully as he yanked me closer.

I wanted him, desperately.

I needed to feel him inside me, hot and hard.

My soaked center met his erection, and I took another long pull of his blood as I lined us up.

He didn't wait for me to finish setting us up—he was already pulling me down and driving into me.

I choked on his blood as he filled me, hard and fast.

I'd had sex with a few humans, but Ronin was nowhere near human.

He was fucking huge.

My mind swam.

My throat closed.

And my body... it moved with his, through no effort or intentions of my own.

He moved.

I rocked.

He dragged his thumb over my clit.

I moaned.

And between his taste lingering on my tongue and the way he felt inside me, I was a goner.

I cried out as I climaxed, my fingers digging into his skin as I lost control on his cock.

He snarled, chasing my release with his own as he filled me with his pleasure.

I closed my eyes, not wanting to look him in the eyes and accept what we'd just done.

Our chests rose and fell rapidly together, one of his hands still gripping my breast possessively. The other was on my upper thigh, and his thumb was still pressed against my clit.

It felt good.

Too good.

Way, way too good.

I gave myself two last deep breaths—and when they were through, I forced my eyes open.

And found him staring at me.

His gaze was molten.

His grip on my breast tightened.

"That was fucking unreal," he said, his chest rumbling with the words.

My entire body reacted to his words, my channel tightening around him while I shuddered.

His eyes slammed shut as his cock throbbed in response.

I wanted more.

I wanted so, so much more.

But he wanted it to be permanent.

And I couldn't give him that. Not when it would cost me my freedom.

So I forced myself to release my hold on him.

He opened his eyes as I eased myself off his erection—and he caught me by the waist when my trembling legs buckled. "Be careful, Tor."

"I warned you," I said, my voice shaking almost as much as my legs. "Obviously the venom affects you pretty strongly. Now, I need to get going." I stepped back, and when my legs held me up, started toward the door.

I heard his growled curse behind me, but I was already moving.

He caught me at the front door, his palm landing on the wood and holding it shut just as I grabbed the knob.

No pun intended that time, either.

The *door*knob.

Door. Knob.

"You said you'd let me go home after I drank from you," I said, without turning around.

My voice was still shaky as hell.

"Going home isn't the same as running away from me." His free hand caught my hip gently, and I squeezed my eyes shut. "Turn around."

I let out a long breath, but reluctantly turned around.

When my gaze met his throat, I didn't lift my eyes, only because I didn't want to.

He tucked his hand beneath my chin and used the light contact to tip my head upward with a knuckle. My eyes met his, and I found his gaze almost as hot as it had been earlier. "I should've listened to you. I'm sorry."

"Even if you had, it would've gone just like that." I gestured toward the kitchen.

His eyes narrowed slightly. "Was it not good for you?" I laughed in disbelief.

Something akin to panic flashed in his gaze.

"It was incredible, okay? You're…" I gestured toward him a bit violently, and he let out a harsh but relieved breath. "I've only been with humans before. You're amazing. That's not the problem."

"Then what's the problem?"

"This!" I gestured between us. "There's way too much chemistry. I don't want a mate, Ronin. What don't you understand about that?"

"All of it," he tossed back. "What more can you want?"

"My freedom!" My voice cracked with the words.

I swallowed a lump in my throat and shook my head, fighting back a few tears.

Ronin didn't say anything.

I wasn't sure what there was to say.

We wanted the opposite things in life, and there was no way we could both have what we wanted.

A tense moment passed, followed by another.

Finally, Ronin said, "What do you want me to do here, Tor? I physically and emotionally cannot walk away from you. Even if I could, I wouldn't."

"I know. Just take me home, please."

He jerked his head in a nod, taking two steps backward before he disappeared into the hallway for a moment. He was back soon enough, with his keys in his hand.

We made our way out to his truck in silence.

And the drive to my house was one of the most awkward experiences of my life.

# four

TORI

I SLAMMED the door shut behind me and collapsed against it, finally giving up on holding back my tears.

They fell quickly down my cheeks, and I dashed them away. I hated crying, as inevitable as it was sometimes.

The house was silent.

Sienna was still at work.

I had left my phone somewhere. Either at the bakery, in Ronin's truck, or at his house. I couldn't remember, and I didn't have the energy to care.

There was a quick knock on the door behind me, and I let out a long breath.

It had to be Ronin.

I gave him a long minute to decide to leave me alone before I finally turned around and opened it.

When I saw what was on the porch, more tears welled in my eyes, for a different reason.

"Damn emotions," I mumbled, bending down and grabbing the box of heart-shaped sugar cookies. They were my absolute favorite thing at our bakery, but the irony of their shape and my situation didn't pass my notice.

There was a note scribbled across the top of the box in what looked like red sharpie.

> I'm sorry this isn't what you want. When you're ready, I'll do whatever it takes to prove I can make you happy.
>
> —Ronin

I carried the cookies to the couch and plopped down on it. I hadn't cleaned up after we had sex, and was sticky in places I hated being sticky, but the sugar took precedent.

The box landed on my lap, and I was biting into a cookie a heartbeat later.

As I took my second bite, I noticed another note on the inside of the box's lid.

> Text me in the next hour or I'll be forced to abduct you again.

His phone number was written beneath the note, underlined, and circled.

I couldn't stop the smile from curving my lips.

He was definitely persistent.

Given the way Madd wouldn't walk away from Love after they met, I figured I was lucky to have gotten even a few hours alone.

I was halfway through my fourth giant cookie—and well on my way to an awful stomachache—when the front door opened.

Too full to get up, I peered over my shoulder, trying to see the front door from the couch.

No luck, though.

If it was a murderer, I was too sick to fight back anyway.

Sienna and Love came rushing in soon enough, and I relaxed into the couch.

Not a murderer.

Though I was relieved, I also kinda wished I'd been right about the murderer thing, just so I could die without losing my freedom to a mate bond.

That was a terrible way to think, though.

Terrible.

I needed psychological help.

Which might buy me a few more days away from Ronin, considering I could probably get myself checked into a hospital of some sort...

Okay, I was spiraling.

That way of thinking was not good.

Not.

Good.

"What happened?" Love demanded.

Sienna walked over to the couch and sat down near my feet, handing me my bag. It was a sporty little crossbody thing, with a pink and white checkered design on it.

I'd paid more for it than I really felt comfortable with, but I didn't have any bills while living with the pack, and it made me so happy that the money seemed worth it.

I clutched my bag to my chest and took another bite of my cookie, just to delay answering her for a few more seconds.

Love gave me an exasperated look, taking a seat on the couch's armrest, next to Sienna.

When I started to lift my cookie back to my mouth, Sienna leaned over and gently plucked it from my fingers.

"Spill the beans, Tori," Love warned.

Sienna's expression was expectant.

I couldn't avoid it any longer.

"Ronin's my fated mate," I said.

They were absolutely unsurprised.

Sienna's eyes narrowed the tiniest bit. "You're not leaving it at that."

Words spewed from my lips. "Fine, he took me back to the stupidly-gorgeous house he's been fixing up on his own and dropped me on my ass in the shower. After he made me scrub my perfume and lotion off, he gave me his shirt and cooked me eggs and bacon."

I continued, "While we ate, I tried to talk him into walking away from me, but he wouldn't go for it. So, I convinced him to give me a few hours to figure my shit out before he comes back in his wolf form to follow me around in a few days so I have more time to figure crap out."

Sienna blinked.

Love blinked.

Their silence only encouraged the verbal diarrhea.

"But he told me he wouldn't let me leave unless I either sealed the bond, drank his blood, or moved in with him. So, I told him I'd drink from him, then I wrestled the sponge from him, then I sat on his lap. And I bit him, and fucked him, and tried to run away, but he put me in his truck and drove me back ho—"

"Wait, wait, wait," Love said, leaning toward me. "Go back."

"I drank his blood?"

Was I playing dumb?

Yes ma'am, I was.

I should've left out the sex bit when I was telling the story, but my mouth was moving faster than my brain.

"You *fucked* him?" Sienna asked, her eyebrows raised high in her forehead.

"Don't look at me like I'm a slut," I said defensively. "Slut-shaming is a thing of the past. I'm an adult woman, and he's technically my fated mate. Even if he wasn't, it's not slutty to enjoy sex. Don't be a judgy bi—"

Love cut me off. "We're not looking at you like you're a slut, Tori. We're wondering how you went from not wanting a mate to having sex with him in the first few hours after you met him."

Oh.

Right.

I sighed. "I don't really know. It was sexy when he was doing the dishes, so I took over. I had a feeling that he was going to lose total control when my venom started working. I tried to warn him, but you know how hard it is to control yourself when you feed from the vein."

Love nodded.

Sienna just grimaced. I didn't know if she'd ever drank from anyone's veins before.

"It's way more difficult when they're your mate," Love added.

"Well, I learned that the hard way," I said.

Love snorted.

Sienna bit back a grin.

I laughed. "Pun not intended."

"What does the note on the box say?" Love gestured toward it.

I read it aloud. "I'm sorry this isn't what you want. When you're ready, I'll do whatever it takes to prove I can make you happy. Ronin."

"*Vex* fits him so much better than *Ronin*," Love remarked.

"No way, *Ronin* is way sexier," I tossed back.

She didn't need to know that I also kept calling him *Alpha*.

Sienna took a bite of the cookie she'd stolen from me, and I looked down at the box to see how many I had left.

My gaze caught on his phone number.

Right.

Needed to text him.

I unzipped my bag, pretty sure I'd find my phone in there. Sure enough, it was sitting inside.

When I hit the button to light up the screen, I found a dozen missed calls, as well as over a hundred new texts.

"Holy shit, the *Wildwood Bitches* group chat exploded." I typed my code in, but ignored the messages. *Wildwood Bitches* was the name the pack's women had given our massive group text thread. That thing was a pain in the ass to follow, but it was a lot of fun too.

"One of the pack's ladies got abducted from a bakery by a smoking hot alpha," Love said.

I bit back a smile.

She shot me a knowing look. "You like that he threw you over his shoulder and hauled you out of there."

"I would never."

"Liar," Sienna teased.

"Okay fine, it was kind of sexy. That doesn't mean I want a mate," I said.

"You used to tell me that it was a waste of time to try to deny a mate bond after you've already met your mate," Love shot back.

"I was right."

"But?" Sienna prodded.

"But I'm scared out of my mind!" I dragged a hand through my wild, mostly-dry hair. "I don't want to be trapped. I don't want to be stuck with anyone else who uses me the way the clan did. It's not like Ronin wants me—he doesn't even know me. He just wants a mate bond. If his sniffer lit up in front of either of you, he'd be just as happy as he is now. And what happens if he gets violent? Or if he doesn't like me? Or if he wishes he had someone else? I—"

"You're spiraling, Tori," Love said.

I groaned. "I know."

"Just take a deep breath in." Sienna carefully took the box of cookies from me. Though I shot it a forlorn look, I didn't fight to keep them.

I already felt like shit.

"A mate bond isn't a trap," Love said. "It's whatever the hell you decide to make it, but it's not a trap."

"Ronin wants us to be together permanently," I argued.

"He can't seal the bond without you, can he?"

I grimaced. "No. But if I try to leave, he'll come after me."

"And if he comes after you, he'll protect you. Which means you can go anywhere you want, rather than being trapped in Wildwood like you are now," Love pointed out.

My eyes widened slightly.

I hadn't thought about it that way.

I hated not being able to leave Wildwood safely... so maybe I could start to see the mate bond as an opportunity.

Or at least just as something other than the end of my freedom.

"Ronin works for the government," Sienna added. "Which means they've looked into his background a ton. He's safe, at the very least."

"You're right," I admitted.

"And you can always get to know him the human way, with dates and stuff."

I nodded, though I was still grimacing.

"So what's really bothering you?" Love asked.

"I don't want my life to change for him," I said. "I love my freedom. Even if he doesn't try to take it away entirely, everything will change. I can't flirt my way around bars. I can't have fun with both the men and women in my pack. Hell, I'll probably have to join his pack, and I don't even know if there are any women in it. I—"

"You're worried about something that hasn't happened yet," Love said. She'd cut me off again, but I didn't mind.

I appreciated the logic she was offering, even if I had a hard time connecting her dots to the ones in my mind.

"How do I not worry about that?" I asked.

"Just start simple. Start with telling him that you understand there's no way out of the mate bond, but you're not willing to change your life for it, so you want to start slow. By dating," Sienna said simply.

"He might not go for that," Love warned.

I sighed again.

Sienna shot her an exasperated look.

"But he might?" Her addition sounded more like a question than a statement, but she wasn't wrong.

"It's too late to get away from him," Love said. "Like you told me, the past is in the past. Leave it there. You're going to be mated now, whether you like it or not. Embrace it, or be miserable. It's your choice."

Sienna smacked her on the leg, and Love feigned offense.

The past *was* in the past, though.

And what good would it do to hold on to it?

I still needed time to wrap my mind around everything that had changed, and make a game plan of my own, but they were right.

I wasn't trapped.

Not yet.

And if I was certain enough about what I was and wasn't willing to accept, I could give Ronin a choice:

Take the bond the way I was willing to give it, or leave.

Something told me I knew his answer, even if I hadn't come up with a real plan yet.

"I'm going to embrace it," I said reluctantly. "Slowly. In my own way. After I take a shower and think about what I want."

My friends didn't look surprised at all by my words.

I put Ronin's contact into my phone with a sassy nickname and sent a quick text, which he answered immediately.

ME

I'm alive

ALPHA

Need photographic evidence

I snorted.

ME

No pictures. Some asshole dropped me in a shower, so my hair's a mess.

ALPHA

Asshole probably hated the smell of your perfume

ME

It was a very light and pleasant smell, actually

ALPHA

As opposed to your natural scent, which is fucking delicious

I bit my lip.

Love and Sienna had migrated to the kitchen and were talking about something unrelated to the incident in the bakery. Though I had the feeling they wanted to keep talking about me, I appreciated that they gave me a little space.

ALPHA

The next time you drink my blood, it'll be from a cup, while I eat you out.

My body flushed.

ALPHA

How often do you need to feed?

ME

You're supposed to be giving me space

ALPHA

You're not on my lap. That's space.

ME

Space equals distance and time

ALPHA

I haven't had you in my arms for over an
hour. There's the time factor.

ME

Ronin.

ALPHA

Tor

ME

Just let me think

ALPHA

Think about my cock while you text me

ME

RONIN

ALPHA

My cock's definitely thinking about you
while you text me

ME

I'm turning my phone off

ALPHA

Fine. I'll try to hold my wolf back to give
you more time. When he's in control, I'll still
have to shift once or twice a day to check
in with my pack.

ME

**Thank you.**

He didn't respond to that.

Maybe he was as bad at handling gratitude as he was compliments.

Hmm.

I'd have to remember that.

I carried my phone and purse to the bathroom, leaving the cookies behind with one last, forlorn look. Considering how sick I still felt from my stress-eating, that was where they belonged.

## five

TORI

I SPENT ages in the shower, giving myself time to breathe and think.

It relaxed me, which made my mind wander.

And when my mind wandered, it made its way back to the time I spent with Ronin in his kitchen.

We hadn't been there for long, but the chemistry had been wild when we basically wrestled for the sponge.

And when he'd put his hands on my hips.

And when his lips brushed my ear.

Goosebumps erupted on my skin as I closed my eyes and let myself live in the memory for a few minutes.

His body against mine.

Mine straddling his.

His erection against my core while I drank from him.

His hands finding my bare ass and my breast while I unbuttoned his pants.

The unapologetic way he'd touched me.

And fucked me.

I stepped forward, resting my head against the wall of the shower. The water fell behind me, and the cold metal of the shower's controls stabbed my sternum, but I ignored them.

If I was choosing what my mate bond would consist of, sex would most definitely be a part of it.

What else did I want?

That was the question.

My friends had a good point about dating like humans. That would help us get to know each other much better.

But... the more we got to know each other, the more attached we would be.

And the more power he would have over me.

And the less freedom I would have.

So getting to know each other and dating were out of the question.

Telling him I didn't *want* to get to know or date him was also out of the question. He'd rebel, or fight back.

But I had to give up ground on something.

There was no way he would accept being mates who got together to have sex a few times a week.

So what if I gave him what he wanted?

Partially, at least.

I could pack my shit and move in with him, but insist on having my own room.

We could just be... permanent roommates who got physically intimate sometimes?

It wasn't ideal, but it would satisfy him while also giving me the space and sex I wanted.

It was a little bit evil, but what was the alternative? Jumping into a mate bond I didn't want? Surrendering myself to an extremely dominant man who would devour my personal identity if I let him? He was so much larger-than-life, he would swallow me whole if I let him.

My mind ran through what my plan would look like.

I would have to tell him I wanted my own space while we got used to each other. And I'd eventually have to come up with a new excuse, or some kind of alternate reasoning for wanting my own room.

But I could handle it.

And if I was careful, he'd never realize that I was keeping him at an arm's length on purpose.

Hopefully.

With my mind made up, I relaxed and let myself enjoy my shower.

*"It's a good plan,"* my wolf murmured. *"Keeps the peace, and protects our independence."*

*"Exactly."*

I wasn't losing my freedom.

Not to Ronin Vex, at least.

## WHEN I FINALLY DRIED OFF, I felt like my old self.

I was making the best of my situation, and everything was going to work out.

I hummed while I dried my hair and threw a few curls in it. I wasn't going anywhere, but the curls would hold through the next day. Since I had to work, it was going to be an early morning, so it would be nice to have my hair done already.

Love knocked on the bathroom door before she went home to her mate. I dropped my curling iron long enough to pull her in for a tight hug.

"Just keep your mind open," she said. "Having a mate isn't so bad. They're actually pretty fun."

"Whatever you say."

She rolled her eyes at me when she stepped back, though her lips were curved upward. "Good luck."

"Thanks."

She slipped away, and I finished my hair.

Sienna was frosting tree-shaped sugar cookies when I stepped out of the bathroom.

My eyes brightened when I saw them. "You baked for me, after a full day of work?"

"You need it." She said playfully. "I put the heart cookies in the freezer, and I'll add these ones when they're done.

I crossed the kitchen to throw my arms around her, squeezing her deathly tight. "You're the best."

"I know."

When I laughed, she squeezed me back. "You know this isn't the end of the world."

"I do. I have a plan, now."

She released me, and lifted an eyebrow at me when I stepped back. "What is it?"

"I can't tell you. You'll say it's ridiculous."

"Oh boy." She resumed frosting her cookies. "Never mind. I don't want to know."

I made a noise of agreement.

But, when I sat down on one of the barstools and picked up a cookie, I found myself talking anyway. Sienna always had that affect. She was just... trustworthy. And even when she disagreed with me, she wasn't judgmental about it.

"I'm going to move in with him so he chills out," I said.

Her eyebrows shot upward, but she didn't say anything.

"I'll tell him I need my own room, to ensure there's plenty of distance between us. We'll just be roommates. He gets what he wants by having me there. I get what I want by putting enough distance between us that he can't take away my freedom."

Sienna's eyebrows raised higher than I'd realized they could possibly go. "Wow."

"Good plan, right?"

She shot me a look that clearly said it was the stupidest plan she'd ever heard.

I took a bite of my cookie.

"What's going to happen when he eventually realizes what you've been doing?" she asked, after a few moments of silence.

"I'll come up with a good excuse."

"He's not a moron, Tori."

"I never said he was."

"No, but he's going to realize what you're doing. He doesn't want a roommate—he wants a *mate*."

"I know. And I'll still be his mate, I'll just do it on my own terms."

She sighed, shaking her head. "You should rethink this plan."

"Probably," I agreed.

But we both knew I wasn't going to change my mind about it.

My phone dinged in the bathroom, so I went back and grabbed it.

There was a new text from Ronin on the screen.

ALPHA

My wolf's getting too restless. Won't be able to stay away much longer.

I studied it for a minute, considering my options.

If we went through with the plan for his wolf to follow me, he'd have a chance to watch me and get to know me a little.

So... that was out.

Very much out.

ME

No worries. I changed my mind about having him follow me

ALPHA

How many times do I have to tell you I'm not letting you go, woman?

ME

Less than you already have

I wasn't refusing you, I just changed my mind.

ALPHA

About what?

ME

I'm going to move in with you. Seems
inevitable, so I might as well get it
over with

ALPHA

And you're still drinking my blood

ME

Yep, no way around that anymore

ALPHA

Good

I'll come help you pack up

ME

K

ALPHA

See you soon

I tucked my phone in my pocket, then headed back to the kitchen. I pretty much always made dinner, and still had the ingredients for that night's meal in the fridge, so there was no point in avoiding it.

Cooking relaxed me, anyway.

I fell into an easy rhythm as I started following the recipe. Soon enough, there was a knock at the door, pulling me out of the sauce I was making while chicken sizzled in another pan.

"It's Ronin," I told Sienna, still whisking the contents of my saucepan.

"I'll get it." She disappeared down the hallway.

My stomach tightened slightly at the thought of him expecting me and finding her.

What if he grabbed her and kissed her?

Or—

Dammit, I needed to cool it.

He wanted me.

That much had been very, very evident.

And Sienna was back in the living room soon enough, with Ronin at her tail. I watched them over my shoulder.

He hadn't put a shirt on, still wearing just the pants he'd changed into after the shower. His shoulders were tense, though, and there was a crease between his eyebrows that told me he was worried.

His body relaxed when his gaze moved over me, sliding up and down over the leggings and cropped tank I'd put on. The pants were black, and the top was a light blue color. I hadn't bothered with a bra, since I didn't have a whole lot in the chest department, and wanted to be comfortable anyway.

"Can you put the cookies away when you get a chance, Tori?" Sienna asked. "I'm going to take a hot bath."

When my gaze snapped to her, she was biting her lip to hide a smile.

"Yep. No problem," I said, rather than calling her out for giving us space, which she was clearly doing.

"Thanks." She slipped into the hallway, leaving us alone.

"I've got the cookies," Ronin said, his voice rumbling as he strode into the kitchen.

I refocused on my sauce.

Shit, it was thicker than it should've been.

At least it wasn't burnt.

I added a bit of water to thin it out, then whisked it in and set it aside, turning to the chicken. "There are racks in the cabinet next to the fridge. Just set them up and slide the cookies on them, so the frosting has time to set," I instructed, not looking away from my food.

He found them, and after checking to make sure they were what I'd been talking about, set up the cookies.

I transferred the chicken to a baking dish, topped it with cheese, and carefully poured my sauce over it. It went in the oven a minute later, and I brushed my hands off on my apron, glancing at the rice cooker to my side.

Twenty minutes.

Perfect.

I'd take the chicken out when the rice was done.

Turning toward the dirty dishes I'd left on the countertop earlier, I halted.

And frowned.

I knew I hadn't cleaned them up…

I noticed the sink running, and when I turned around, found Ronin already scrubbing them.

Dammit.

I mean, I wasn't bummed not to have dishes to do. That was nice.

But still, dammit.

He wasn't supposed to inject himself into my life by helping me. That wasn't part of my plan.

I'd adapt, though.

Somehow.

I grabbed the last few dirty dishes, taking them to the sink too. "I'm pretty sure we already had a fight about doing the dishes today."

"A disagreement, maybe. But I'd say it ended well."

My mind flashed back to the way I'd sat on him.

Yeahhh… *well* was an understatement.

My face warmed.

"And the disagreement was about you making a statement that if I cooked, you got to clean. You cooked for yourself and Sienna, so I'm cleaning."

"I cooked for all of us," I corrected. "Including you."

His gaze warmed. "Then you have no grounds for arguing against me washing the dishes."

"You're a pain in my ass, Alpha."

His lips curved upward wickedly. "Good."

I leaned my back against the cabinets, turning away from him.

"The food smells incredible. Thank you," he said, continuing with the dishes.

"You're welcome."

"Do you enjoy cooking?"

"I do. I love trying new things, so I always plan a variety of meals for me and Sienna. She likes it too, but she's not as passionate about having variety as I am."

He nodded.

"How many people are in your pack?" I asked.

"I have six wolves. Each of them has close contact with werewolves around the world, so any of them can fly to a location and quickly put together a team of shifters we trust when necessary."

Huh.

"So there are only seven of you? Are any of them women?"

"No. The female werewolves in the government have their own team. They prefer to work alone," he said.

I didn't really blame them.

"Will your wolves be upset that you found me?" I asked.

"Jealousy is likely, but not anger or irritation. If there was an easy way to find a mate, we would all have been paired off a long time ago."

His comment nudged the part of me that didn't like knowing he would've been happy with *any* woman. There was nothing special about me to him; I was just a warm body that fate had declared compatible.

And I really didn't like that.

"Do you expect me to join your pack?"

"At some point, yes." His honest answer was appreciated, even if I didn't like it.

"I like my current pack," I said.

"You'll like mine too."

I flashed him an annoyed look, and he met my gaze steadily.

A long moment passed before I finally ripped my eyes away from his, staring at the stove.

After a moment of silence, I grabbed a towel and dipped it in the sink's falling water, wetting it. I wiped down the countertops, cleaning up the rest of my mess while Ronin did the dishes in silence.

We were quiet as we worked together until the rice cooker beeped to let me know it was done.

I pulled the food out, and Ronin opened drawers and cabinets until he had enough plates and utensils for all three of us. I put Sienna's plate together and headed to her room to deliver it—giving her a dirty look and taking her playful smile in return.

When I made it back to the kitchen, Ronin was setting two full plates at the table, across from each other.

I stared him down for a moment before I took my seat.

He waited for me to sit too before he picked up his utensils.

We continued staring at each other as we ate, our gazes flicking down to our plates when absolutely necessary.

When our food was gone, he set his utensils down and cleared his throat. "That was delicious. Thank you."

"You're welcome."

A moment of silence passed before he spoke again. "This feels like some kind of cowboy standoff, Tor."

I couldn't suppress a grudging smile. "It does."

"So let's fix it." He rested his forearms on the table and leaned toward me. "Tell me how to make this easier for you."

"I would if I could," I said honestly.

"Why don't we just start with being friends?" he asked. "A mated couple should be friendly, first and foremost."

I nodded. "Alright. Friends."

"Good. Now, give me your plate. I'll wash the dishes, then we can start packing."

As much as I wanted to protest, I couldn't.

Not if I was going to follow through with my plan.

So, I agreed.

## RONIN

I CARRIED both of Tori's boxes through my front door, her duffel bag hanging off my shoulder. She'd glared at me when I tried to take everything, so I let her carry her backpack. It had a few electronics in it and not much else, so it wasn't too heavy.

My body was a fucking livewire.

My wolf was alert, and preening at the idea of having our mate in my bed.

Holding her.

Touching her.

Kissing her.

I couldn't wait.

Heading toward the master bedroom, my eye was so set on the prize that I missed the first time she called my name.

"Wait, Ronin," Tori said from behind me. "I don't want to share a room. We need to get to know each other first."

I stopped in the doorway of our room.

*My* room.

My shoulders tightened anyway.

"Don't get all tense. It's not a big deal. We'll still be living in the same house—I just need space until I'm ready for the next step in the relationship. Moving in together is already a big deal."

I let out a long breath and turned to face her. Her expression was calm, but decisive.

*"Why did she offer to move in at all if she wanted to live separately?"* my wolf asked suspiciously.

*"I don't know."* As much as I disliked the idea, I didn't think turning her down outright would do anything but start another fight. "I'm working on the master bathroom right now. Haven't had time to finish a spare room yet."

She frowned.

Her forehead creased, then smoothed. "I'm sure I'll be fine in a room that's not done."

"No. If you don't want to share, you take the master."

"I'm not kicking you out of your own room."

"Then you'll have to share it with me."

Her gaze was steely.

Mine was too.

She let out a long breath. "Fine. You sleep in your wolf form, though."

My wolf liked that idea tremendously.

I, on the other hand, did not.

But if she was letting me have my way with living in my room, I had to let her have her way too.

So, I jerked my head in a nod.

And finally, she followed me into our room.

I carried her boxes into the closet, since I'd never bothered buying a dresser. When she didn't follow me, I looked over my shoulder.

Her lip was between her teeth as she checked out the room, studying everything without getting too close to anything.

My gaze lingered on her.

She looked damn perfect in my space.

My wolf rumbled his agreement.

"Do you approve?" I asked her, forcing my attention back to the box as I opened it up.

"It's gorgeous," she admitted.

My wolf rumbled again.

"Just don't look at the bathroom," I said.

She laughed, and of course, headed straight there.

I didn't have to follow her to know what she'd find. It was a wreck. The plumbing and electrical were done, and the drywall was up, but I hadn't textured or tiled anything.

"Well, it's a really good size," she called from the bathroom. "And I like the shower. It's gigantic."

She joined me in the closet a minute later, and immediately started helping hang her clothes. "No dresser?"

"Nah, they're pointless."

"It saves time when you don't have to hang all of your clothes."

I made a noncommittal noise. "I've always had plenty of time."

She watched me for a few minutes before she spoke again. "What's it like to be immortal?"

I frowned. "*You're* immortal."

"Yeah, but I'm only twenty-three. I don't feel immortal yet."

Huh.

"It's long," I admitted. "You learn to rely on the people you're close to just to stay sane."

"Do you have family?"

"No. I lost them in the war. A lot of wolves did."

She continued studying me.

I didn't stop her. As long as she liked what she was seeing, the more she looked at me, the better.

"I don't have family either," she finally said. "Except Love and Sienna. And things have been different with Love ever since she mated with Madd. She's happy, but I miss her."

"I've lost a handful of friends to mate bonds. The relationship changes, even when you don't want it to."

"Exactly."

We unpacked the rest of her stuff in relative silence. Her scent filled the closet, and was more than enough to keep me at peace.

"Well, I have to work in the morning," she finally said, straightening and dusting her ass off. I'd looked at it more than enough to know it wasn't dirty. "I'm going to call it a night."

I pulled my phone from my pocket and checked the time. "It's barely eight."

"I'm a baker," she reminded me. "I work early."

"I'll get up to drive you."

"Thanks, but I have a car. And you have plenty of work here." She gave me a small smile. "Goodnight."

And with that, she headed off to bed.

I watched over my shoulder as she turned off the lights after a stop in the bathroom, then slipped into bed in her leggings and tank. The thin top had been driving me crazy since I walked into her house. Her nipples were visible through the fabric, and that made me want to touch them.

And taste them.

And fuck them.

But I stayed where I was.

*"Something is definitely up,"* my wolf rumbled. *"She's agreed to everything far too easily after the way she tried to run away from us earlier."*

*"Maybe she really did just need time to process everything."*

He grunted.

I didn't believe that either, but I'd give her enough space and time to settle before I pushed her any more than I already had.

# *seven*

## TORI

I SOMEHOW MANAGED to avoid Ronin for the better part of about a week. We spent a little time together while I cooked and he cleaned, but otherwise, we left each other alone for the most part.

I worked, and picked up extra shifts to stay busier.

He made some progress on the house, and pressed his lips together when he wanted to call me out for working excessively.

It was actually fairly peaceful.

And his wolf was a sweetheart. He was just a big, snuggly teddy bear. I would definitely never complain about letting him keep me warm.

Ronin didn't try to convince me to meet his pack.

I didn't ask him to, or bring up my pack.

It wasn't awkward, though. It was strangely civil.

I was starting to think I might actually like having him as a roommate when the seventh evening came around.

As much as I hated being hungry, I hadn't commented to him about my hunger since it started creeping up on me a few days earlier. Feeding would mean having sex with him, and I liked having sex with him way too much to keep things friendly.

And I wasn't sure how to advance that part of our relationship without making him think I wanted more.

So, I'd been ignoring my ever-obnoxious horniness and forcing myself to continue on like I wasn't struggling not to throw myself at Ronin.

The last bite of my dinner was halfway to my mouth when my stomach rumbled.

Loudly.

I paused for a moment.

Ronin's eyes—which were always on me when we were together—narrowed.

I took my bite, and chewed.

He watched me.

I pointedly didn't look at him as I set my fork down on my plate and brushed absolutely nothing off the front of my sports bra, to give myself something to do.

From the corner of my eye, I saw him set his forearms on the table and start leaning toward me.

Shit.

I needed to do something, pronto.

*"Shift,"* my wolf murmured.

"It's been way too long since my wolf's taken control," I blurted. "She wants to run. And she still hasn't met your wolf."

Ronin's chest rumbled. His wolf would be excited by the prospect of running with his mate—and hopefully, distracted by it. So he wouldn't question my growling stomach.

I would have to do something about it, of course.

I'd have to feed from him.

And it might lead to sex.

But at least going on a run would buy me a little time.

"We'll shift after you drink from me," Ronin said.

*"Crap,"* I whispered to my wolf.

*"It's probably a good idea."*

I hurried to reply, "That's not necessary. I'm fine."

"You're not shifting while you're hungry." His words were blunt, his expression hard enough that I didn't think he'd be changing his mind. "If you're not ready to have sex, you can drink from my wrist."

My face flushed.

Hell, my entire body did too.

My fangs descended, on top of that.

I shouldn't have been so flustered at the idea of having sex with him, but dammit, I was. The way we'd both lost control of ourselves the last time had been so good.

"Fine," I said.

He stood long enough to step over to the chair beside mine, and sat down.

I let out a slow, unsteady breath.

When he gave me his wrist, I took it reluctantly.

My fingers pressed lightly into his skin as I lifted his arm toward my mouth. My fangs throbbed at the scent of him. I didn't think I'd ever get tired of the way he smelled.

"I'll keep myself under control this time," Ronin said.

I couldn't suppress my snort.

His responding grimace made me smile against his arm.

And finally, I bit him.

My moan filled the room as his taste flooded my mouth.

Ronin gripped the edge of the table with his free hand, the one in my grasp forming a fist.

He managed to remain in his seat while I drank quickly, taking deep, hard pulls.

Me?

I wasn't doing nearly as well at fighting it.

My desire was hot and thick, my need overwhelming.

And fighting it while his blood was in my mouth?

It was nearly impossible.

I found myself reaching for him.

Taking his free hand.

Pulling it off the table.

And dragging it to my center.

He groaned, his fingers pressing against my clit over the front of my leggings.

My hips rocked.

I pulled his hand to the waistband of my pants.

Claws sliced through the tight fabric, cutting my thong too.

Hot, rough fingers found my slick center.

And finally, he touched me.

He wasn't gentle, but he wasn't cruel.

The pressure was hard, but not painfully so.

He worked me, and my legs opened wider, desperate sounds escaping me as he dragged me to the edge of my pleasure.

Finally, he slid a thick finger inside me, his thumb still on my clit, and I lost it.

I cried out against his arm, my fangs releasing his skin as my climax cut through me. My chest rose and fell rapidly, my body jerking and rocking desperately against him.

His movements slowed as I came down from the high—but he didn't remove his fingers.

Finally, I opened my eyes.

And found his fixed on me.

Not on my lower-half, but on my face.

On the way I gripped his arm for dear life, and the blood that was probably smeared on my lips after the way I'd released him.

His gaze finally dragged down me, and stopped at the apex of my thighs.

I let mine follow—and my entire body clenched when they halted.

My bright yellow leggings were torn down to the centers of my thighs, with strips of fabric straining and curling in random bits.

His hand was slick and shiny—with one of his his fingers lost inside me, and his thumb on my clit.

He circled it slowly, and I sucked in a breath.

His gaze went back to my face, though mine remained fixed on his hand.

The finger inside me grazed something sensitive, and my hips jerked again.

"You're fucking gorgeous," he said, his voice low and smooth enough to make me shiver. "I want to watch you climax on my hand again without your venom clouding my mind, Tor."

His thumb slid over my clit, and I sucked in a breath. "Alright." The word was soft, but not uncertain. Not even a little.

Ronin's thumb continued moving torturously slowly.

My hips jerked.

His finger curved, finding that spot inside me, and I shattered.

My cries cut through the air again as I lost it, riding out my pleasure on his fingers. His chest rumbled in satisfaction, and I leaned back against my chair, needing something to rest against.

His gaze was hot, and remained fixed on me. Though his fingers slowed and stopped, his eyes didn't move.

Mine didn't either.

We remained exactly where we were as my breathing evened out.

That... hadn't been part of the plan.

Granted, I'd never been much of a planner.

And it had felt *incredible*.

"Thanks," I finally said, and wrapped my fingers around his gigantic wrist. When I pulled lightly, he removed his hand from between my thighs.

"Don't thank me." He lifted his hand to his mouth and dragged his tongue alone the slick pad of his finger. His chest rumbled again, more fiercely. "I'll be fucking my hand to the image of you until the next time you let me touch you."

My body flushed, and I eased my legs closed. The movement didn't do a damn thing to cover me—just dragged his attention back down.

Where it lingered.

"You can buy me new leggings," I said, finally easing myself to my feet.

"I'd rather you wear these ones." He didn't stand up.

A glance down at him showed a tent in his jeans—a very large one. It looked like it might be painful, but I wasn't about to offer to take care of it for him. My mind was still spinning from the orgasms he'd given me, and the taste of his blood was still on my tongue.

"That's not up for debate," I said, finally turning around.

His chuckle filled the room as I walked away from him— and the breeze I felt on my backside told me he was seeing plenty of skin there, too.

Despite the situation, I didn't feel a shred of discomfort about the way he'd seen me. And that might have concerned me more than anything else.

. . .

I CLEANED MYSELF UP, then put on a pair of soft sleep shorts before I headed out to the living room. They swayed against my ass with every step.

Ronin was wiping the countertops clean, having already finished washing the dishes. His jeans were still tented, but I acted like I didn't notice that.

His gaze slid over me slowly, but I ignored it as I walked to the back door. He abandoned the countertops and caught me as I reached it, pulling it open before I had the chance. Rather than protesting, I stepped outside.

His hand landed on my waist, and he guided me to the side of a large tree. When I looked back at him, I found his gaze scanning the forest, his forehead creased.

"What are you doing?" I asked.

"Making sure my pack isn't around. I don't like you stripping out here where any of the bastards could see you." His attention didn't return to me, for once. "Shift behind me. You should be hidden for the most part."

Wow.

I'd shifted a dozen times with my pack before, and had definitely flashed more than my fair share of men and women. It was part of being a werewolf.

But was it worth a fight?

No, it was not.

So I drawled, "Yes, Alpha."

He looked back at me as I grabbed the bottom hem of my sports bra.

I stopped.

And lifted an eyebrow.

He let out a long breath and focused back on the forest. "I just fucked you with my fingers. Don't know why you're worried about letting me see your tits. We're *mates*, Tor."

"*Room*mates," I corrected.

He made a noise of disagreement.

I huffed. "Fine, we're mates. But I'm still adjusting to everything. Any idea when you'll be done fixing up my room?"

"I'm getting close on the master bathroom. Laundry room has to come afterward. Your bedroom can be third."

"The laundry room is functional," I protested.

"There are leaks. I'm not risking mold."

"Fine." I peeled my bra over my head and stepped out of my shorts. "My wolf is just as uncertain as I am. Make sure yours doesn't overwhelm her."

"He would never hurt his mate," Ronin growled back.

"Of course he wouldn't, but you're clearly an alpha. My wolf isn't."

"*I can handle him,*" she murmured back. "*Don't worry about me.*"

I would always worry about her, though. We'd been through too much dark shit with the clan that created us.

"He's more laid-back than I am. He'll take care of her," Ronin said, his anger gone.

I had no choice but to trust him.

Particularly when my wolf's magic rolled through me.

I shivered, and my spine elongated as my body changed instantly. My wolf's paws met the packed dirt of the forest floor, and my mind slipped into the strange pocket that existed between us.

Ronin's eyes were on her as she shook out her fur. Though she stayed where she was, she studied him curiously.

"May I?" He held his hand out in front of her, clearly asking if he could pet her.

She hesitated, and her thoughts went to me. *"Are you okay with it?"*

*"I just let him fuck me with that hand, girly. You've got the freedom to do whatever you want with him."*

I felt her humor before she finally stepped toward him, stopping when her head met his palm.

He crouched down in front of her, still dressed as he slid his fingers into her fur and rubbed her head lightly.

"I've waited centuries for you. Thank you for surviving for me."

If I'd been in my human form, my throat would've swelled.

He knew what I'd been through, at least on a basic level. He knew that I'd suffered; that I had survived.

My friends and I never talked about it. It was far too painful. But I suddenly wanted to share it with him, if just so he would wrap me in his arms and tell me I was strong.

Of course, I couldn't act on that desire.

Or at least I *wouldn't*.

But that didn't change the fact that I wanted to, desperately.

My wolf stepped closer to him, nearly purring at the feel of his hands in her fur.

*"He's strong,"* she said.

*"Extremely."*

*"We could've done worse."*

*"Undoubtedly."* As much as I hated to admit it, that was the truth.

After a minute, Ronin reluctantly let go and stepped back. "My wolf says it's his turn."

Mine purred louder.

Her gaze remained on our mate as he stripped his shirt off —followed by his pants.

So did mine.

Though we'd had sex, it had been frantic and under the influence. So, I'd never actually *seen* him naked before.

And hot damn, the man was a masterpiece.

Thick, chiseled muscles.

Monstrous thighs.

Hard cock basically saluting me.

And those arms...

Yumm.

*"Your mouth would be watering if you were in charge right now,"* my wolf teased me lightly.

*"No point in denying that."*

She chuckled inwardly.

And continued staring for my sake as Ronin tossed his clothes onto the porch—followed by mine—and shifted.

A heartbeat later, his wolf was in front of us. He was just as massive as I'd expected, with dark fur that matched the shade of his human's hair, and the same electric blue eyes.

*"Finally,"* he rumbled, taking in my wolf's appearance. *"Stay there. I want to look at you."*

She lifted her head higher as he circled her slowly, as if she were prey.

I couldn't help but worry about her just a little.

He was a damned giant, after all.

*"Fucking perfect."* The approval in his voice was so thick, it would've made my knees a little weak if I'd been in control.

He stepped up against my wolf's side, brushing his fur against hers.

My wolf eased away, and he didn't follow her, giving her space.

*"You lead a pack?"* she asked.

*"A small one,"* he confirmed. After a moment's pause, he added, *"My human wants me to ensure you know it's the only small thing about us."*

My wolf chuffed—the closest she could get to a laugh.

I snorted.

*"How fast are you?"* she asked. Her tail was wagging slowly. She was hopeful and excited, and that made my heart soar.

*"Faster than you."* His teeth snapped playfully in the air.

She chuffed again, then took off into the trees.

And despite the shittery of our situation, and how much I would've liked to get out of it, I was glad we were stuck.

Because it made her happy.

...which meant I might need to rethink everything about my plan.

Yikes.

That would be tomorrow's problem.

# eight

## RONIN

OUR WOLVES RAN and played in the forest for hours before they finally made their way back home. Their footsteps were slow, their sides all but glued together as they moved. It was the middle of the night, but I didn't give a damn about the time.

My wolf was with his mate.

*I* was with my mate.

The world as I knew it could've been ending, and I would've been so blissed out, it didn't matter.

*"Did you hear her mention being roommates?"* my wolf asked me, as we neared our house.

I thought about it. *"When we were in the kitchen?"*

*"Yes."*

*"I guess."*

*"That's how she's been acting. Like you live together."*

*"We do live together."*

He snorted. *"Like you* only *live together. Like you're room-mates, not mates."*

Ah.

*"She's still warming up to me,"* I said.

*"And she'll still be warming up to you two decades from now if you let her. She's keeping you at an arm's length on purpose."*

*"That's not a bad thing. Getting to know each other for a while before sealing the bond is healthy."*

*"Are you getting to know each other, though?"* my wolf asked.

He reached the house as I considered the question, ending the conversation as we shifted back.

Tori's sexy, bare ass was stepping into the house, her clothes dangling from her fingers, by the time I made it up the porch steps.

I caught the door just before it closed—and in time to hear her call out, "I'm taking a quick shower before I go to bed. It's an early morning tomorrow."

"You've worked every day this week," I said, the words coming out grumpier than I intended.

"Baker life is a bitch!"

The bathroom door shut and locked behind her.

Dammit.

I raked a hand through my hair.

Maybe my wolf had a point.

## A FEW MORE DAYS PASSED.

The more I paid attention to how quickly she walked and turned away for me, the surer I was that she was avoiding me.

But I had no damn idea what to do about it.

I couldn't ask her to work less hours. That seemed like a dick move, and I needed her to like me.

I also couldn't force her to warm up to me faster, or to share my bed in our human forms.

And I was already moving at a damn snail's pace with the house. Eventually, she would realize I wasn't making much progress on the master bathroom. The sooner I was done renovating, the sooner she would move out of our bedroom.

Other than working slowly, I wasn't sure how to get more from her without pushing too hard.

## ON THE EIGHTH day of my personal hell, Madd pulled up behind *Coffee & Toffee & Cake* while I was sitting outside.

Was I doing anything worthwhile?

Not a fucking chance. It was nearly painful to walk away from my mate while she worked day after day. It wasn't like she needed the money—I'd give her everything she needed, and so much more.

But I sat.

And waited.

He sat in the front seat of his truck and stared at me for a moment before he finally raised an eyebrow in my direction.

I grimaced.

He crossed the parking lot and studied me from above. A minute passed before he finally said, "You look like shit."

I grunted. "Hadn't noticed."

He let out a long breath, then lowered himself to the concrete beside me.

Another minute went by before he said, "Mate problems?"

I made a noncommittal noise.

"Blood wolves are a pain in the ass."

That, we could agree on.

"Love tried like hell to convince me to let her go after we met," he said.

My gaze jerked toward him. "She did?"

"Yep."

"Damn. Never would've guessed."

"I abducted her. We made it work." His gaze lingered on the forest, and I looked out at it too. "You know they've been through hell."

"I know. I'm trying not to push her."

The bakery's back door opened, and Love strode out. Her chin-length waves bobbed around her face, and Madd's entire body relaxed as he looked over and took her in.

She plopped down on his lap without bothering to ask permission. "Hey, Arch."

Fuck, I wanted that from my mate.

The comfort.

The confidence.

He dragged her to his chest, his arm wrapped possessively around her. "Hey, Vee." He kissed her cheek, and her lips curved upward.

I would legitimately kill for what they had.

"What are we talking about?" she wondered.

"Difficult women," Madd said.

I grimaced.

"Tori's being difficult, huh?" Her voice was knowing.

I didn't confirm or deny anything, though. I wasn't going to break my female's trust. Particularly not with one of her best friends.

"Got any advice for him?" Madd asked.

She grinned. "Tori likes to have fun, and loves trying new things. She also feels trapped in Wildwood. Take her somewhere new, and she might open up to you."

It...

Well, if it worked, it would be a great idea.

I just wasn't sure it would work.

"You think she'll go on a *vacation* with me? The woman has worked every day since we met."

Madd snorted. "Love pulled the same shit when we first met."

"Yeah, it's easy to get more hours," she said. "And our boss is cool. If you bring up a vacation, Tori's schedule will find itself magically clear. She's wanted to get out of here for ages, but it's not safe for us. Especially her."

"Why 'especially her'?" My words came out a growl.

"Easy," Madd warned, his chest rumbling slightly. His arm had tightened around Love's middle, and her fingers dragged lightly over his arm, as if comforting him.

"I'm fine," she told him, before looking back at me. "You'll have to ask Tori. It's her secret to share. But believe me, a vacation will work. If she says she can't get the time off, call Zander Villin. His mate owns the coffee shop. Madd knows him, so I'm sure you do too. If our boss insists on Tori taking time off, and there's a vacation scheduled, I can't see her saying no."

The Villins were a trio of demon brothers insane enough to make a life out of hunting vampires who killed humans. I wouldn't call myself friends with them, but we were friendly.

"Thanks." I dragged my hand through my hair.

"Good luck," Madd said, as he and Love stood. They were in his truck and driving away soon enough, leaving me staring out at the forest.

It would be fun to go on vacation with my mate.

Especially because she needed to drink my blood soon.

My lips curved upward, slightly wicked.

I couldn't let myself push her... but I could seduce her with the freedom she'd have if she agreed to be mine.

If she was allowed to treat me like nothing but a roommate, I was allowed to play dirty.

# nine

## TORI

I DIDN'T BOTHER SUPPRESSING my grimace at the pain in my feet as I hobbled out of the bakery.

But said grimace vanished immediately when I halted in the doorway.

And as I stared at the beautiful man sitting on my junker car's hood with two duffel bags at his feet. He had a pair of sunglasses on his face, and a ballcap over his head.

My mind scrambled to come up with a reasonable explanation for the sight in front of me.

He was moving out?

He was moving my stuff out?

He was... leaving me?

Yeah, right.

I had nothing.

I let out a long breath before I finally forced my feet to move again.

Shit, they hurt.

My grimace returned as I walked, trying to move at my normal pace so he wouldn't realize how exhausted I was.

"What's wrong?" his words were low, but there was an edge to his voice that made my stomach tighten.

And my fangs descend.

I really needed to get back on a better feeding schedule. But, avoiding him and drinking his blood didn't seem to be compatible goals.

"Just tired," I said, forcing a smile.

"Are we in the habit of lying now, Tor?"

My smile vanished. "Fine, I feel as bad as I look. Are you leaving me? If so, can we get it on with?" I gestured toward his duffels in irritation.

His forehead wrinkled. "What the fuck? I'm not leaving you. We're going on a vacation."

I blinked.

That was unexpected.

The wrinkle in his forehead deepened. "Why would you think I'm leaving you?"

"What vacation?" I ignored his question.

My heart was pumping fast at the mention of going somewhere.

Anywhere but Wildwood or Scale Ridge would be amazing.

"The theme park with the big castle. I figured we'd spend a few days on the beach afterward, and—"

"Let's go." I was already walking toward my car.

"I'll drive."

Any other day, I might've considered arguing. But considering my long shift and my long few *weeks*, I didn't even want to drive a little bit.

I tossed him the keys, and he caught them effortlessly. The clicker didn't work, so I waited outside the car while he unlocked the door, then hit the button to open mine.

"Damn," he said, looking around the vehicle as he turned the ignition.

"It's a shithole. I know. The bakery doesn't pay well." I shut the door behind me.

And didn't mention that I'd spent all of my money buying Sienna a much more reliable car a month earlier. She had protested, but the tears in her eyes and the appreciation in her voice affirmed my knowledge that she needed it.

My savings account was slowly making a recovery, anyway.

And my car *did* work. It just smelled weird and made odd noises *while* it worked.

"It's fine. Needs a good cleaning, that's all." He put it into reverse, and winced at the grinding noise. "And maybe a tune-up."

"I'll sell it as soon as I have the money to buy something more reliable. I'm not attached to this hunk of junk," I said, kicking my shoes off and propping my socked-feet up on the dash. A groan escaped me at the sudden relief.

"You've been working a lot," Ronin said, pulling out of the parking lot.

"Yep." I tilted my head back against the seat, focusing my gaze out the window. "What inspired you to whisk me off on vacation?"

"Love."

I blinked.

My body tensed.

He wasn't proclaiming...

Holy hell.

He was, wasn't he?

But we barely knew each other! And I sure as hell wasn't the girl who—

"Your friend Love," he clarified, apparently picking up on my sudden change of mood. "She told me to seduce you with a vacation."

I sighed inwardly.

Of course she had.

"Those weren't her exact words," he clarified. "The seduction part was my take on it."

Dammit.

If he tried to seduce me, he would sure as hell succeed.

"Seems like it's working," I finally said, my gaze still on the forest as we drove.

"Don't be frustrated. You've been pushing me away."

"I've been avoiding you," I corrected. "Love is the one who told me there's an art to avoiding your werewolf. I'm trying to figure it out."

He chuckled. "She avoided Madd *really* well."

"I know." My voice was glum.

But despite my exhaustion, I was still excited.

Because I was getting out of Wildwood. Going somewhere new.

"Try not to sound so happy, Tor."

Though my lips curved upward the tiniest bit, I said, "I'm too tired to be happy. What time does the plane leave?"

"It's on my phone." He grabbed it out of the cup holder and handed it to me. My thumb lingered over the numbers, uncertain about the passcode, and about asking for the passcode.

That was kind of intimate, wasn't it?

I didn't want to give him *my* passcode, after all.

"It's eleven-eleven. My older sister used to text me at 11:10 every day to make sure I remembered to make a wish. Sometimes the messages would come through midday, and sometimes late at night—but the only days she ever missed were the days her pups were born. And I was waiting in the hospital to meet them, those days."

I bit my lip and typed the code.

Though I was dying to ask for more information, I needed to be a steel trap.

No interest.

No questions.

No—

"Why did she stop?" The words slipped out.

I had no self-control when I was interested in something.

"She died in the war."

I glanced his way, and found his expression... bittersweet.

"She led a long, happy life, but she fought alongside her mate and sons. Almost all of the female wolves did. None of them would listen to reason. One of her three sons survived. Vander. He's my beta, and my closest friend," Ronin admitted.

"I'm sorry," I said, biting my lip again.

I definitely shouldn't have asked. Now, he seemed... like a person.

Someone with emotions.

And that made it harder to keep my distance from him.

"It's not your fault." His hand brushed my knee briefly before he lifted it to the steering wheel. "The tickets should be in the airline's app."

He wanted a subject change.

Thank heavens.

I found the app and pulled up the information. We were plenty early—and looking at the tickets made me even more excited.

"Love mentioned something about your blood," Ronin added. "I need to know as much as possible, so I know who and what to look out for while we're out of Wildwood."

Right.

That was logical, even if I didn't like it.

"I affect vampires a little differently than Love and Sienna. I'm more potent, I guess. No one knows why. My scent draws them in from much further, and my blood tastes better, too."

"Damn."

"Yep." I closed my eyes for a moment, and let my face fall the way it wanted to.

"Did they treat you worse because of it?"

"Of course they did." The words slipped out of their own accord.

I was too tired and too comfortable to keep secrets from him, even though I logically knew I needed to.

He was silent, but when I looked over, his fingers had tightened on the steering wheel.

That small sign of his anger was enough to spur me into saying more.

"I kept Love and Sienna in the dark about as much as I could. They didn't need to know, and I didn't want to talk about it. I just wanted to get out. I just wanted..." I trailed off, not sure how to finish the sentence in a way that wouldn't hurt Ronin.

And as much as I didn't want a mate, I still didn't want to hurt him. It wasn't him I didn't want. It was the commitment. The permanence. The trap.

"Freedom," he said quietly, finishing my thought for me.

I let out a long breath. "Yeah."

"It's not what you want to hear, but you could be much freer as my mate than you could without me," he said.

My forehead wrinkled, though my gaze had returned to the forest we were driving through. "How do you figure that?"

"With a sealed bond, vampires wouldn't be able to take you for your blood without taking me to feed you. No one creates or takes a blood wolf to drink from them once. You're an easy, stable food source that doesn't age and tastes great on top of it. A refillable plate of steak."

"Thanks," I drawled, not wanting to admit that I could see his point.

"I'm serious, Tor. You're steak—and the vampires want you. But if we seal our bond, they can't have you. Not without taking me too. And if they take me, the wolves will rain hell on them. Hundreds of other supernaturals will tag along, backed by the government. No one would be stupid enough to hurt you if you were mine." A heartbeat passed before he said, "*When* you're mine."

My heartbeat picked up a little with everything he added.

*If we seal our bond, they can't have you.*

*Not without taking me too.*

*No one would be stupid enough to hurt you if you were mine.*

He added, "And for the record, we have more money than we can spend in a dozen immortal lifetimes. We'll replace your car when we get back if that's what you want, or we'll get it fixed. We can go wherever we want, we can *do* whatever we want. If that isn't freedom, what is?"

I didn't have an answer for him.

Not one I could talk myself into believing, at least.

Because he was right.

Mating with him meant money.

Safety.

Security.

Companionship.

Vacations.

*And if that wasn't freedom, what was?*

The thoughts rolled around in my mind the rest of the way to the airport, and as we made our way through security and to our gate.

They lingered up until I fell asleep with my head against Ronin's shoulder, and his arm around my waist.

And damn it all to hell, I dreamed of a life with him.

A life of freedom, and fun.

If I wanted to keep my distance from him, I was going to have to work my ass off.

And potentially, lie to myself.

Yay.

WARM FINGERS BRUSHED my hair off my face just before I felt a bit of a jolt beneath me.

I wrestled with my groggy eyes.

"We just landed," Ronin said, and kissed my forehead.

The soft gesture made me warm.

"I slept like the dead," I mumbled, my mouth dry and weird-tasting.

"I noticed. Here." He slipped a water bottle in my hand. "I don't want you dehydrated before we make it to the beach."

"Yes, Alpha," I grumbled.

He chuckled. "If I was your alpha, I wouldn't have let you drool on me for the past few hours, Tor."

I jerked my head off his shoulder, and my eyes widened when I saw the wet patch on his shirt. "Holy shit. I'm sorry."

"Don't be. That was the best flight of my life." He finger-combed a few wild strands of my hair down. "And now you look like you've been properly fucked, too. Just imagine what everyone who sees us will think this wet spot on my shirt is."

I poked him in the chest. "You are *terrible*."

He laughed—a full-bellied laugh that made my whole body warm.

I like that sound more than I should've.

That didn't seem like a good sign.

His grin was wide, and relaxed. "I'll take that as a compliment."

We were off the plane soon enough, with both of our bags hanging off his shoulders even though I'd tried to take one. The nap hadn't energized me as much as I would've hoped, so I was sagging pretty badly. My steps were slow, and my feet still hurt too.

We walked through the airport for what felt like forever.

At some point, he looped a finger in the waistband of my leggings so he could pull me along. I was so exhausted that I actually appreciated the help.

"You can go ahead of me," I said.

He rolled his eyes at me, and didn't bother responding.

"I'm serious. I don't know what's wrong with me—I feel like shit."

"You're ignoring your hunger."

I blinked, still moving at the same pace. "I am?"

"You are," he confirmed.

Dammit.

Since he'd mentioned it, I did remember ignoring my growling stomach at work...

"You need to eat before you feel hungry. We're setting a routine while we're here. And we're doing whatever the hell we have to, to make you comfortable enough to be okay with that."

My whole body flushed.

I loved his no-nonsense tone, even if it made me want to strangle him a little.

A little strangulation wouldn't really hurt, would it?

I was going with no.

And no matter how much I tried not to let it get to me, his, "whatever the hell we have to" had my mind going back to that first day, in his kitchen.

The way he'd felt inside me.

The way he'd taken me, while I drank from him.

The way—

I needed to get my mind out of the past already. Time was running out to come up with a new way to put distance between us. I needed more ideas, stat.

## TORI

I DUG my phone out of my pocket and texted my friends while Ronin dragged through the airport by the waistband of my leggings.

ME

> Teach me the art of avoiding a werewolf, Love

Please

I'm drowning here

LOVE

> LOL You already avoided him about as much as I avoided Madd

> And you always told me you'd stop trying to avoid your mate after you'd already met him. There's no running from him now.

ME

> Stop turning my own logic against me, woman

You're supposed to be on my side!

LOVE

I'm on the side of love

And yes, that terrible joke was intentional

SIENNA

What happened? Why are you drowning?

LOVE

Isn't he taking you on vacation?

ME

Yeah, He was waiting outside the bakery with two bags when I got off work. I assume one has my clothes in it. When he mentioned a certain theme park, I was in the car and ready to go too fast to ask questions.

Or make an excuse

SIENNA

You've always wanted to go there!

ME

I know. Did you tell him that bit too, L?

LOVE

No, I just told him he should ask you to go on vacation with him if he wants to soften you up

It's working, isn't it?

ME

OMG I hate you

Of course it's softening me.

I'm like fucking frozen butter.

LOVE
How does one fuck frozen butter?

SIENNA
LOL

ME
I'm leaving

SIENNA
Not without an explanation for the butter
thing you're not.

I huffed, and earned an amused look from Ronin. My attention snapped back to my phone as soon as I was sure he
couldn't read the messages over my shoulder.

ME
Frozen butter melts fast when some other
frozen things take forever. It doesn't make
much sense now, but it was logical when I
wrote it out

SIENNA
Hahahahaha

LOVE
Maybe he's worth melting for ;P

SIENNA
Aww

ME
STOPPP

Just tell me how to avoid him

LOVE
Sorry to be the bearer of bad news, but I
don't think you can at this point

SIENNA

I'll send cookies when you're back from
your vacation

LOVE

I'll send flowers, just so you can see how
possessive he gets when he thinks some
other guy is flirting with you

ME

No flowers. It's not a damn funeral.

...is it?

I need help

Must re-freeze the butter

SIENNA

Have you ever tried refrigerating melted
butter? That shit is never the same

TORI

YOU GUYS WERE SUPPOSED TO MAKE
ME FEEL BETTER

Sienna sent a gif of someone hugging someone who was crying.

Love sent one of someone patting someone else on the back.

Ronin tugged hard on my leggings, pulling me toward him, and my attention jerked back to reality as my side brushed another woman's.

Whoops.

"Thanks," I said, slipping my phone back into my pocket. It vibrated a few more times, but I'd read the messages later.

When I wasn't in the middle of a busy airport.

"No problem." He used the opportunity to release my leggings and slip his fingers between mine, claiming my hand instead.

I'd never held hands with a guy before.

I'd made out a few times, and had sex almost as many... but never held hands.

It was foreign, but nice.

Comfortable.

Warm, too.

I liked it.

My arm pressed lightly against his as we made it to baggage claim and waited for the duffels. I found myself leaning against him while the baggage carousel drove circles until it finally spit out our bags.

He released my hand long enough to grab both of them, and was back at my side a moment later, recapturing my hand and towing me toward the rental car area.

Soon enough, our bags were on the back seat, and we were driving toward our hotel.

Ronin recaptured my hand while he maneuvered the roads. My body warmed at the contact, and I didn't pull away.

I still didn't want a mate.

But I could enjoy holding his hand, right?

"What's the plan for today?" I asked him, while my eyes traveled over the new landscape. It was early in the morning, and the morning sun was shining down over the scenery in a way I loved.

"We're checking into the hotel first. After you feed, we'll go out to breakfast, and explore the city. After lunch, I figured we'd spend a few hours at the beach."

I bit my lip, excitement lighting me up. "Sounds like fun. We can skip the feeding part, though."

He shot me a "fuck no" look before refocusing on the road. "You eating isn't up for debate."

Dammit.

"You'll have more energy when you're properly-fed, anyway. And more fun."

I couldn't argue against that.

Not when I knew he was right.

We reached the hotel soon enough, and checked in quickly. I slipped into our room behind Ronin, my gaze moving over the space.

It wasn't ginormous—I didn't think Ronin was the kind of guy who'd throw a shit-ton of money at the most expensive room he could find—but it was comfortable. There was a huge tub in the bathroom, and surprisingly enough, there were two beds.

"I thought you'd force me to snuggle with you," I remarked, as he set one bag down on the foot of each bed.

"Nah. I figured I've pushed you enough for one day, and I'm tired of sleeping in my wolf form." He tugged his shirt over his head, and my eyes immediately fixed on his bare chest.

Hot damn.

"I'm going to take a quick shower before you feed from me. Always feel dirty after plane rides." He gave me a quick smile, and with that, stepped into the bathroom.

My attention followed him into the bathroom, and lingered on the doorway when he left it standing open.

It was a clear invitation.

I bit my lip and took one quiet step to the side so I could watch as he unbuttoned his pants and pushed them down those gigantic thighs.

His ass was unreal. A perfect, tight bubble.

My fists tightened as I fought the urge to touch him.

My body was warm, and I was wet between my thighs just at the sight of him.

There was no denying that I wanted him, badly.

And I was so tired of ignoring it.

I pulled my phone out and looked at my messages.

SIENNA

Everything's going to work out <3

LOVE

You've got this! We believe in you!

Despite their words of encouragement, I forced myself to turn away after Ronin stepped into the shower, and I unzipped one of the bags.

The plethora of bright colors told me it was mine.

My lips curved downward when I caught a glimpse of a bright orange shade I didn't think I owned. I slipped the fabric out, and stared down at a pair of brand new leggings with tags on them.

The tags showed the symbol of an expensive brand. The same one my favorite pair of leggings were. Mine were from a thrift store, of course.

But he must've noticed me wearing them.

And remembered that I told him he needed to replace the ones he'd torn the last time I fed on him.

My face flushed at the reminder.

I set the fabric down—planning on wearing it to show him I appreciated the gesture—but in the corner of my eye, caught a glimpse of an identical tag.

That piece of clothing was in my hands a heartbeat later.

A bright yellow sports bra, in the same style I preferred.

I dropped that on top of the orange leggings, and grabbed the next piece of clothing.

And the next.

And the next.

Emotions welled in my throat by the time I finished unpacking everything.

It was all new.

The fabric was soft and buttery.

In the colors and styles I loved.

They were things I never would've bought myself, even if I had the money to spend—and the gesture meant so damn much to me, I didn't even have the words to say.

I opened the pockets on the bag, and found more new things.

I let out a long, shaky breath, and started folding the clothes.

My mind raced, though.

Ronin was a good man. A kind man, too, despite his obvious dominance and alpha-ness.

He cared about me.

And while I didn't want a mate, it wouldn't hurt to be friends.

Or more than friends.

I folded two more pieces of clothing before my mind was made up. Then, I abandoned the rest on the couch, and strode into the bathroom.

Though I was calm outwardly, my heart raced on the inside.

There was no going back from what I was about to do.

The room's shower was large, and tiled beautifully, but I didn't pay it any attention.

Not when its glass wall revealed the thick muscles of Ronin's shoulders as he washed shampoo from his hair. Or the bubbles rolling down his chiseled back, drawing my eyes to his ass.

Damn, what an ass.

I gave myself a moment to take him in before I started peeling my bra over my head and called out, "Do you think the shower's big enough for two?"

He looked over his shoulder, and his gaze moved slowly, hungrily, over my bare chest. "Always."

I stepped out of my leggings, abandoning them on the floor with my bra as I stepped inside.

He made space for me beneath the hot water, turning to face me but keeping his hands to himself.

His erection was thick and hard, jutting out toward me.

My lips curved upward, and I wrapped my hand around him.

His groan was low and animalistic, his hands clenching at his sides.

I slowly dragged my hand down his length.

He swore as he throbbed in my hand, hot and heavy. "Let me touch you." His voice was strained.

"After I get you off, I'm all yours."

I stroked him slowly again, taking one of his hands and lifting it to my breast. He didn't hesitate to grab me, his grip rough but not painful.

The other, I lifted to my waist as I worked him.

He squeezed the hell out of my hip before he walked me backward. My shoulder blades hit the shower's wall, and water dripped down my body as he pressed me against it.

His hand left my hip, and he took a small step to the side, swearing as I rolled my grip lightly over the head of him.

"Fucking hell, I don't want to know who taught you how to do this," he gritted out.

I cried out loudly as his fingers slipped between my thighs, dragging over my clit.

The pressure was perfect.

The slight roughness of his callused fingers was, too.

My hips rocked, and I worked him faster.

He did the same.

Until finally, he snarled with his climax. His touch grew rougher and harder as he lost it, dragging me over the edge with him. My cries were loud and desperate—and he rewarded them with even more pressure on my clit, making everything feel more intense.

"Holy shit," I breathed, chest rising and falling quickly as I came down from the high. His pleasure was rolling down my abdomen and core, but I felt too good to care.

"You're incredible." His growl made me hot all over again.

His fingers between my thighs helped with that too.

"Thanks." I closed my eyes, leaning against the shower. "We should do that again sometime."

"If that's your way of giving me permission to touch you whenever I want, you're going to need to be clearer about it. There'll be no turning back from that. Not for me."

Desire clenched in my abdomen. "That's a lot of pressure for one decision. I'm going to need some time to think about it."

"Take all the time you need, Tor." His fingers were still between my thighs—and when I opened my eyes, his attention was hot, and focused entirely on my body.

"You can't look at me like that," I said.

"Like what?"

"Like I'm the sexiest thing you've ever seen."

He chuckled, the sound low and rich. It gave me intense goosebumps. "You are the sexiest thing I've ever seen. Or touched. And when I finally get my mouth on you, you'll be the sexiest thing I've ever tasted, too."

My body heated. "No one's ever gone down on me before."

His chest rumbled with approval. "Then I don't have to kill anyone for having you on their tongue."

"You're not going to kill someone for sleeping with me in any way before I was yours."

"You've always been mine. I just wasn't there to claim you yet." His hand abandoned my core just long enough to grab my hip again. It was slick with my desire as he turned me around. "I want your ass against me while I fuck you with my fingers. I want to see what it'll look like when I take you from behind."

Ohhh shit.

My breasts met warm tile my back had been pressed against, and he lifted my hands one by one up to rest on either side of my face.

When his hand found my thighs again, his fingers slid over my clit, then my entrance.

I sucked in a breath when he teased me for a moment, before finally slipping a thick finger inside me.

My breathing grew shallow at the sudden feeling.

It had been too long since he was inside me—my body wasn't used to it.

Ronin stepped up against my back, his chest hot and hard as it pressed against me. His free hand adjusted the position of my ass, until his gigantic cock was wedged between my cheeks. Somehow, it only turned me on more.

"How does that feel?" His thumb dragged over my clit while he slowly worked his finger inside me.

"Good."

"We can do better than good, Tor." He slid his finger out, and added another one before he pushed back inside me.

A gasp escaped me at the sensation.

He teased my clit. "Better?"

"Yeah." The word was breathless.

He tsked his tongue. "Not what I wanted to hear."

His fingers left me again—and when he slid them back inside, he'd added a third.

My knees knocked together as he dragged his knuckle against the wall of my channel, exactly where I needed him.

I cried out as the orgasm hit me, hard and fast.

His thumb worked me slowly, his fingers in place inside me. "That feel good?"

"Incredible," I moaned.

"My cock will be better. Tell me you want me."

"I want you." The words flew out of my mouth so fast, he chuckled.

"I'm yours, Tor." He slid his fingers out of me, and slowly dragged them up my abdomen. My body ached for more—for him—but he wasn't in a hurry.

Slowly, his slick fingers circled my nipples one by one.

Then, they slid over my breasts.

"What are you waiting for?" I growled, when he continued teasing me.

"You wanted time to make that decision. I'm giving you time."

I turned around, still pinned between him and the wall. My breasts met his chest, and his cock throbbed against my abdomen. "I don't need to make a decision to fuck you."

His eyes were still hot.

His slick fingers slid down my back, wrapping around my ass and squeezing before it slipped between my ass cheeks.

The slow drag of his slick digits over my back entrance made my thighs clench.

"Alpha," I gritted out.

"Tori." He continued teasing my ass with his fingers.

"*Ronin.*" The word was harsh.

"I'm not fucking you until you can promise me that you belong to me as much as I belong to you." His words were simple, but not soft.

He wasn't going to budge on that.

"I can't promise you that." My hips arched as his finger dipped into my back entrance.

Holy hell, he was going to make me climax again, and he was hardly trying at all.

"Then you don't get my cock." His free hand slipped between us, and I swore when he found my clit again.

"You don't get to manipulate me," I argued.

"Demanding equality is a far cry from manipulation, Tor."

He rocked his thumb against my clit, and I nearly climaxed.

I was so, so close.

"Dammit, Ronin!" I cried out. "Stop touching me."

His hands went still immediately.

His cock throbbed against my abdomen. "Yes, *Alpha.*"

I wasn't an alpha.

My wolf was even less of one than me.

But damn it all to hell, he was making a point.

I was in charge of what happened between us. I made the calls—and he listened to me, even when he didn't want to.

I wasn't an alpha, but I had one at my beck and call. And that was kind of the same thing.

My mind went back to the clothes on the couch.

To the way I'd stripped down and stepped into the shower.

I was tired of fighting myself to keep my distance from him.

And honestly?

I wanted more.

So, I let out a slow breath.

Finally, I said, "My body is yours. I can't promise you anything else right now, but my body is yours."

He stared at me for a moment.

A long, long moment.

My stomach tensed at the possibility that he wouldn't take it. That he would reject what I'd offered. That he would—

"That's good enough for now." He pressed against my clit again, moving his thumb slowly, and I lost it.

Detonated like a damn bomb.

My cries were frantic as I rocked against him, and he didn't disappoint.

The tip of his finger left my ass, parting my thighs and bracing me against the wall as he slammed into me.

I choked on the sounds of my pleasure with the sudden sensations.

Full—I was so full.

Desperate—I was so desperate.

My cries escalated as I rocked against him while he thrust into me, dragging out my orgasm and setting off another one.

The most intense one I'd ever experienced.

I screamed his name as I climaxed on his cock, my channel squeezing the hell out of him.

He roared, flooding me with his pleasure while I did.

I was boneless when it finally came to an end, and collapsed in his arms. He held me up effortlessly, though his body trembled slightly.

"You good?" I managed, still short on breath.

"Amazing." He mumbled the words against my hair, adjusting my position without putting any space between our bodies. "I had no idea sex could feel like that."

"Neither did I," I admitted.

"Thank fuck for that," he rumbled. "If another man could please you the way I can, I'd be obligated to hunt him down."

"You would not." I bumped his ass lightly with the back of my heel.

Damn, that was a thick ass.

I still wanted to touch it.

"Have you slept with anyone in Madd's pack before?" he asked.

I could read between the lines to figure out what he was really asking. "No, I've never had sex with a supernatural before. And you're a hell of a lot bigger than any of the humans I was with."

His shoulders relaxed.

"Have you slept with anyone in Madd's pack?" I asked.

"No. The only women I've ever been with were human, and only a handful of them throughout the centuries. The loneliness peaks every five or six decades, and I needed something to remind myself that I was alive for a reason."

My stomach clenched, hard. "Sleeping with women felt like a reason for being alive?"

He snorted. "No. My wolf would never let me enjoy sex with a female who wasn't my mate. Getting them off reminded me that I was waiting for a woman I could please whenever I wanted. And yes, I know it's twisted."

It wasn't, though.

He'd been lonely—and loneliness made people desperate.

"I get it." I slipped my hands into his hair, burying them in the soft, wet strands. "Your body is perfect, for the record."

He adjusted his grip on me, changing the angle a bit. When he did, his cock hit me differently, and pleasure made my spine arch.

"Bite me, Tor." He squeezed my ass. "Now."

A laugh escaped me, but I lowered my lips to his shoulder, and bit him.

We were both lost to the lust a heartbeat later.

# eleven

## TORI

WE EVENTUALLY MADE it out of the shower. Ronin ordered early lunch, since we obviously hadn't made it out for breakfast, while I blew my hair dry and threw a few curls in. My makeup came after that, and I felt like a new person by the time I slipped out of the bathroom in one of my new outfits. The food had just arrived, so it was perfect timing.

"Well?" I put a hand on my hip and gestured to my new clothes.

"Sexy as hell," Ronin said, approval thick in his voice. "The only way you could look better is if you took everything off."

I made a face at him, and he grinned as he opened the boxes of food up on the bed. There was a table, but neither of us bothered sitting down at it.

His shoulders were more relaxed than I'd ever seen them.

There was a contentedness in his expression that I'd never seen before, too.

I had to bite my lip to hold my smile back when I realized *I* had done that. *I* made him feel good. The larger-than-life alpha, tamed by a blood wolf.

So much for being at the bottom of the food chain.

We sat across from each other on the bed, and devoured our food in relative silence. It was peaceful silence, though. Relaxed silence.

I was done before him. "So, a little exploring, then the beach?"

"Mmhm." He kept eating.

"I didn't see a swimsuit in the bag."

"Side pocket of mine." He gestured toward his own duffel.

It felt wrong to go through his bag, but I ignored the feeling and stepped over there, unzipping the pocket.

A snort escaped me when I saw the first bikini.

It was neon pink, and the tiniest swimsuit I'd ever laid eyes on.

Then again, I hadn't worn a swimsuit since before the clan took me, and I'd been way too young back then to pay attention to what other people wore.

But still, the thing was tiny.

"Really, Ronin?" I lifted the strip of fabric by the string it was connected to.

His grin was wicked. "If we're going to the beach, we might as well enjoy the view."

I flipped him my middle finger, and his grin widened.

The swimsuit beneath it had our country's flag spread across the breasts and crotch, and it was just as small as the first one. Maybe smaller. "Somehow, it got worse."

He laughed, and I couldn't bite my lip to suppress my smile.

The third swimsuit was slightly more modest. It was shaped similarly to a sports bra, though the fabric was much thinner and smaller. The top was half bright blue, half bright green, and the bottom was the same, but the colors were in opposite positions.

And it was a thong.

"You nearly had a stroke at the thought of your packmates seeing me shift," I remarked. "I wonder how you'll feel when the human guys on the beach see me in this." I lifted the thong.

His grin vanished.

"Your funeral." I grabbed the matching top, along with a beach towel I'd noticed in a stack in the bathroom.

"Fuck," he muttered. His next bite was much more violent.

· · · ·

WE DROVE around for a few hours before we made it to the beach. Our hotel had a private one, so we changed into our suits there before heading out on the sand.

Ronin cursed under his breath when he saw me in my swimsuit—then put his hand on my ass.

He was trying to keep me covered, though he couldn't resist taking a handful every few steps.

While it was a beautiful day, the beach was empty. Dozens of chairs were spread out on the sand, but there wasn't a soul in any of them.

My eyes caught on a chair to my far right.

Well, there was one soul in one of them.

An elderly man was asleep on one of the lounges, with the umbrella over him so large that I could barely see him.

"Guess we don't have to worry about you getting jealous," I remarked.

"Thank fuck," he muttered under his breath.

I looked over the white sand, and the crashing waves. It wasn't calm—but it wasn't crazy, either.

Then again, I'd never seen the ocean in person before. I wasn't the right person to ask about the state of it.

I couldn't peel my eyes off the expanse of water. It was unlike anything I'd ever witnessed. Vast, beautiful, and wild. Like the forest, but with more energy.

*"It's nice here,"* my wolf murmured.

*"It is,"* I admitted.

*"Maybe we should talk Ronin into moving here. He would do it for us."*

*"You say that like we're going to be stuck with him permanently."* My words were half-hearted.

Her wolfy smile was soft.

She didn't tell me there was no way out of a mate bond, but she didn't need to.

*"He's good for you,"* she said instead. *"He's not afraid of change, and he travels a lot. Plus, he treats you well."*

*"Shh. Don't hit me with the truth."*

She chuffed, but didn't bother trying to convince me.

Being in denial was better than feeling trapped for me.

"Want to sit down?" Ronin checked, waiting for me to take the lead.

Maybe I liked it when he let me play alpha for a minute.

"Not yet." I strode toward the waves. The motion pulled my ass away from him—so when he caught up to me, he took my hand and threaded his fingers through mine.

We tossed our towels on lounge chairs on our way to the water, and walked in together.

Of course, as soon as the water hit my toes, I screeched and jumped backward. "Holy fuck, that's cold!"

Ronin snorted. "Did you think it would be warm?"

"Yes!"

He grinned. "It's not."

I huffed at him, and took a reluctant step back to his side, taking his hand again.

He squeezed mine lightly, and I braced myself when the second wave washed over our feet.

It was just as cold.

We waded further out, and slowly, my body grew numb to the iciness.

That didn't stop me from gravitating closer to Ronin's side, or clinging to his hand while I waited (and waited, and waited) to get used to the cold.

I'd probably freeze to death before I made it out, but hey, at least I was out of Wildwood, and *living* for once.

When we made it out far enough that the water was up to my chest, we stopped for a few minutes.

"Are you sure you want to do this?" Ronin asked.

"Of course I'm sure. Just cold." I paused a moment, then asked, "How are you not cold?"

"I am. This is just the first time I haven't been hard since the day we met in the bakery, so I'm trying to enjoy it. The cold has some perks."

I laughed, *hard*.

Pun intended.

Ronin gave me that gorgeous grin of his and pulled me into his arms.

I cuddled up against him, shivering a bit violently. "I pictured this going differently."

"Which part?" His hands moved lightly up and down my back.

"The beach thing. I've never been before," I admitted.

He squeezed me. "We'll have fun despite the cold. Most people just sit out on the beach and nap or read anyway."

"Do you nap, or read?"

"I don't usually go to the beach."

"Well, that's sad."

"Never had anyone to go with before." He squeezed me again, a bit more firmly. "Now, I plan on enjoying the view, and napping with my mate."

That did sound nice.

Especially after the ice bath we were having.

"First, I have to give you the complete beach experience," he added.

I frowned.

"How do you do that?"

His expression grew mischevious for all of a heartbeat—before he said, "Hold your breath!"

Then dunked me under the water with him.

I came up gasping for air, with icy water dripping down every damn part of me. "Ronin!"

He laughed. "If you don't have salt on your skin and hair, you haven't done the beach properly.

"Says you." I splashed water at him, and he ducked out of the way just in time to avoid it.

He splashed back, and I went under just to avoid the small wave.

Of course, I regretted it as soon as the ice water hit my face, but it was what it was.

Ronin grabbed me by the waist, scooping me out of the water and tossing me into the air. I laughed loudly on the way back down—and soaked him again when I hit the water.

As silly as it was, our game continued until my teeth started chattering.

Then, we made our way back to the sand.

Ronin tossed me over his shoulder a few yards before we escaped the water, and I laughed as he jogged me over to our chairs. He tossed one of our towels over the lounge chair —it looked pitifully small on there—before he collapsed, pulling me down with him and draping the second towel over me.

His chest was deliciously warm against mine, so I snuggled in closer. He pulled me up onto his chest, his arms around my back and holding me tight.

My shivering calmed down quickly, though it took a while to really warm up.

Both of us relaxed more the longer we laid there. The sound of the waves was almost supernaturally calming, and I loved it so much I didn't have words for it.

Maybe my wolf was right about moving to the beach.

But I'd miss Love and Sienna too much. So, maybe I just needed to go on vacation more often.

I wasn't sure how much time had passed when I finally peeled my head off Ronin's chest and peered up at him. His breathing was even, so I wasn't sure if he was awake or not.

His gorgeous blue eyes collided with mine immediately, though, and his lips curved upward. "The beach looks good on you."

"It looks good on you too." My voice was soft and playful.

The man blushed a bit.

Damn, I loved how bad he was at taking compliments.

My eyes caught on his lips, and lingered there.

We'd done a hell of a lot, but we'd never kissed.

And I wanted to know what he tasted like.

So I lifted my mouth to his, and kissed him.

The movement caught him off guard, but he recovered quickly and slipped his tongue into my mouth. His hands wrapped around my mostly-bare ass, and he used his grip to pull me further up his chest.

I tilted my head, giving myself better access as my hands tangled in his hair too.

He kneaded my ass while our tongues warred, discovering every inch of each other's mouths. His erection was hard against my core—and he moved me against it.

The friction wasn't anywhere near enough to get me off after the morning we'd had, but it felt good anyway. And more than that, it was fun.

We were making out on an empty beach. With the ocean crashing somewhere behind us. While—

Something hit my back, and I jumped, yelping when the sudden motion threw me off balance. I rolled right off Ronin, too quickly for him to catch me, and hit the sand hard enough to knock the breath out of me.

"What the hell?" Ronin growled. "You okay?"

"I'm fine."

He looked me up and down to make sure I was, then grabbed a foam shoe off the sand. It must've been what hit me. He stood, and was storming across the beach a heartbeat later.

"Shit," I muttered, pulling myself to my feet and rushing after Ronin.

I had long legs, but nowhere near long enough to catch up quickly to a pissed male werewolf.

"Who the fuck throws their shoe at a woman?" Ronin snarled, said shoe clenched tightly in his fist as he held it up.

As I got closer, I realized who he was talking to.

The elderly man who'd been sleeping.

Oh boy.

Something told me ancient werewolves weren't taught to respect older people the way humans were as children.

I jogged faster, wrapping an arm around my chest to stop it from bouncing. My breasts weren't big, but hey, they could still bounce a bit.

"It's a foam shoe. Hardly going to kill someone," A grumpy male voice said. "Umbrellas aren't walls. Get a room if you want to—"

"I don't give a damn what it is, you don't throw it at a woman," Ronin snarled.

"I'm so sorry," I said quickly, talking loud just in case I needed to drown out Ronin's words. His free hand caught my hip when I stepped up next to him, and he gripped tightly.

When I plucked the shoe from his hand, it took a second, but he finally let it go.

I put on a sugary-sweet smile and made my voice as cheerful as possible. "We should've gone back to our room. It was rude to let things get that far on the beach. Thanks for interrupting when you did. Here's your shoe back." I set it down next to the other one, which was still on the sand. "And I'm sorry about my mate. Werewolf guys are a little overprotective." I winked at him.

The man looked taken-aback by my attitude, which was sort of the plan.

Charm 'em thoroughly enough to make an escape. It had saved me from a hell of a lot of extra pain when I was with the clan.

"We'll be going now. Thanks again for being so understanding." I gave him one last smile, then grabbed Ronin's arm and literally dragged him away from the man.

Though his jaw was clenched and there was anger in his eyes, he didn't dig in his heels or try to stop me.

Soon enough, we were away from the man's sight, and I let out a long breath. "You can't go batshit on an elderly human, Ronin."

"He could've hurt you."

"With a foam shoe?"

"You fell off the damn lounge chair!" He tossed a hand in the direction of the beach, pulling his arm out of my grip and pacing the lobby we'd stepped into.

"It was my fault. We shouldn't have been making out like that in public," I protested.

He covered the space between us in two steps and took my face in his hands, looking me dead in the eyes. "He could've thrown *anything*, Tor. You could've easily been injured."

"But I wasn't," I pointed out.

"But you could've been," he growled.

"But I *wasn't*."

"We're not arguing about this." He grabbed me by the waist and tossed me over his shoulder.

## TORI

RONIN DEPOSITED me on the bed and stepped into the bathroom, slamming the door behind himself.

I sighed as it shut, and kneaded my temples with my fingers.

We hadn't brought any of our stuff down to the beach, including our shoes, so nothing had been left behind but the towels. And according to the signs I'd seen, someone was paid to pick up those towels.

Which meant I didn't have an excuse to slip out of the room.

After a long moment, I finally went looking for my phone, and found it without much of a hassle.

Knowing Love would respond immediately, and would have some advice (though it would probably be questionable), I sent her a message.

ME

What do you do when you and Madd
disagree about something?

LOVE

Depends on the situation. What kind of
something?

ME

He got super insanely overprotective and
didn't like that I said it was unreasonable

LOVE

Ah

Yeah, that happens

It'll pass

ME

I don't know if it will

LOVE

The possessiveness usually comes down
to some kind of fear. Werewolf guys spend
their whole lives looking for their mate, so
it's natural for them to be afraid of losing
her, whether to another guy or to
something else. Remember how Madd
was when I got a cold last month?

ME

Yes

He was insane

I've never seen a grown man sit at his
woman's workplace for so long just to
keep an eye on her cold.

LOVE

I know. He was worried about me. And despite the weirdness, did it really hurt to let him take care of me that way?

ME

I guess not

LOVE

Mates take care of each other. When you're paired with an alpha, sometimes taking care of him requires letting him be ridiculous just because it will make him feel better.

ME

But Ronin literally yelled at an elderly human man

LOVE

Okay, I'm going to need the full story on that one

ME

We thought we were alone on the beach. Things got steamy. Old guy threw a foam shoe at me to tell us to can it. Ronin stormed over and yelled at him, so I hurried over and smoothed things out. He's mad that I intervened.

LOVE

Damn, go Vex

Madd would definitely lose his shit if someone threw something at me. He probably wouldn't yell if it was a woman, but a man would 100% piss himself after the verbal destruction. The guy could've hurt you

ME

It was a foam shoe!

LOVE

It's not about the shoe, Tori. He could've thrown anything at you

Vex is upset because he didn't protect you. If someone had tried to hurt you, they would've succeeded.

ME

He can't protect me from everything

LOVE

If you don't want to get locked in a house for the rest of your life, I'd recommend not saying that to a male werewolf

ME

I guess I should go talk to him

LOVE

If you're not trying to avoid him anymore, I would definitely recommend it

Whatever you do, good luck!

ME

Thanks

I dropped my phone on the bed, then walked to the bathroom door and tried the knob.

It was locked.

Damn, he was really upset.

And I could hear the shower running, which would be my in.

I knocked on the door and called loudly, "I was told there's always enough room in that shower for two people."

"I need a few minutes," he growled back.

"Fine, I'll just sit on my ass on this highly-uncomfortable tile floor until you're ready to talk to me," I declared. "My butt will probably be sore for days, and—"

He yanked the door open.

The man was naked, with water dripping down his body in ways that made him look absolutely delicious.

I didn't let myself stare at him, though.

And I wasn't sure what to say.

So, I stepped toward him and wrapped my arms around his neck, rising up on my tiptoes as I hugged my sandy, bikini-clad body against his warm, strong, wet one.

A moment passed.

Ronin's arms finally wrapped around my back and slowly tightened around me, pulling my body harder against his.

His nose met my neck, and he inhaled slowly, breathing me in.

The tension in his shoulders and grip told me not to step back. The hug wasn't as good as a conversation probably would've been, but it was helping him.

And I still wasn't sure how to start a conversation.

An apology?

It wouldn't seem genuine, and I didn't think he was the kind of guy who would take a half-assed apology well.

Maybe telling him I understood would work?

I didn't really understand though.

Hopefully the hug would be enough.

He squeezed me roughly before releasing me and striding back into the shower.

My gaze followed his ass, before I followed him into the bathroom, then into the shower.

His back was to me.

I needed to say something...

And that thought propelled words from my mouth.

"I'm sorry. Not for stopping you from threatening an old man—but for hurting you when I did. That's not what I wanted. I can't say I understand why you went off on him, but I know you're usually level-headed. I trust that the reasoning behind it makes sense to you."

He let out a long breath. "I don't fucking know the reasoning. Something hit you, and it scared the shit out of me. I know it was just a shoe, but it could've been worse. You could've been hurt. I could've lost you."

"That sounds like the reasoning to me. It scared you."

"I wasn't scared. I was just..." he trailed off. "Fine. Fuck. I was scared."

"Your instinct was to defend me. I guess I should be glad you didn't wolf out and tear into that guy." My voice was softer, and slightly playful.

He sighed. "It did cross my mind."

I stepped up behind him and wrapped my arms around his middle. He turned around, pulling me to his chest instead of his back.

Tilting my head, I looked up at him and found emotions storming in his eyes. "I can't lose you. We haven't even sealed the bond—if I lose you, I'll lose my fucking mind. I can't do life alone again. Not after I've had you."

His words were vulnerable.

My throat swelled.

I didn't want a mate... but I didn't want him to be hurting, either.

Or scared.

"That's not going to happen, Ronin. You're not losing me. I'm on vacation with you, for fuck's sake."

"You'd go on vacation with any man willing to protect you from the vampires you come across, Tor."

He had me with that one.

"All I have of you is your body, remember?"

Dammit, he had me with that one, too.

"That's technically true, but—"

"Don't bullshit me." His voice wasn't rude, but it wasn't kind, either. It was rough, like the rest of him.

I let out a long breath. "Fine, you're right."

"I know. I'm sorry for losing my temper. Right now, I'd like some time alone with my thoughts." He released his hold on me, stepped away, and turned his back.

My throat swelled thicker.

My emotions made my eyes burn.

I grabbed a towel and left the room quickly, closing it behind me.

Tears continued stinging my eyes, and I swiped at them angrily.

I was not going to be hurt because he wanted space from me.

He was the one who dragged me to his house, then gave me no choice but to move in with him.

He was the one who forced me into our shitty roommate situation.

He was the one who insisted that we stay together!

And now he was angry that I didn't care about him the way he cared about me?

Screw him!

Not in a sexual way, either.

Anger made my movements harsh as I grabbed his t-shirt off the bed and pulled it over my head. I picked up my phone, and a keycard to the room, then stormed out.

Well, I didn't *really* storm.

I had to close the door quietly so he didn't realize I was leaving, so storming wasn't really an option.

But still, I walked angrily.

I called Love on my way to the elevator, and she answered immediately.

"I don't think a phone call so soon after our conversation is a good sign."

"It's not." My words were clipped. "I hugged him, and told him I was sorry and that I trusted there was a reason he flipped out. He told me he couldn't handle losing me. Then, he brought up that I've told him I'm not really his—and he told me to leave!"

There was a moment of silence. "*Leave*, leave? Like, get out of the hotel room, leave? If he kicked you out of the hotel room, you know I'll be up there to kick his ass in a heartbeat."

My anger fizzled slightly.

Just slightly.

"Well, no. I did leave the hotel room, but he told me he needed time alone with his thoughts." I stabbed the elevator button, and watched the numbers light up as it rose toward me.

"That makes me feel better. No ass-kicking required."

We both knew Love couldn't actually kick Ronin's ass. But, I was pretty damn confident she could point to just about anyone's backside, and her mate would take care of the kicking part.

"So what are you the most upset about?" she prodded. "Because you sound hurt, and you're usually pretty damn hard to hurt."

I bit my lip while my mind rolled back to the conversation. Tears stung my eyes again. "I told him he wasn't losing me, and he didn't believe me. He basically said I'm only here for the sex, Love. That I don't want him, when I think I've made it really damn clear that I do."

"You've made it clear that you don't want a mate for a while now." Her words were gentle, but honest.

More tears stung my eyes, and I wiped them away in frustration as the elevator dinged.

There were people in it—which was just fucking great.

All of them stared at me as I stepped in.

I knew I looked like shit. I was crying. My swimsuit had soaked Ronin's t-shirt in awkward places. My hair had dried in weird stringy, salty tangles.

"I've got to go," I said to Love.

"Wait, Tori, I—"

I hung up as the elevator doors closed.

The next minute went by slowly.

I swear, it felt like an hour.

The bell finally dinged again, and I stepped out.

My eyes caught on the hotel's small bar, and I beelined it in that direction. It was mostly empty, so I wouldn't be bothered too much in there.

One side of the room had an actual bar with stools, while the other had couches, chairs, and coffee tables. A few of the stools were taken, so I tucked myself away in an empty corner with a couch, chair, and table. When someone came up and asked if I wanted anything, I barely glanced at the menu before I ordered the drink at the top, and the dessert at the bottom.

My phone rang again a minute or two later, and I sagged against the couch as I looked down at the screen.

Sienna.

Love must've called her.

I reluctantly lifted the phone to my ear. "Please don't try to make me feel better."

She laughed softly. "You know that's not my specialty. I don't think that's any of our specialties."

I relaxed against the couch I'd taken. "Love told you what happened?"

"She thought someone who also didn't have a mate would know what to say more than she did."

I sighed.

She was quiet.

I finally said, "Alright, tell me what you think."

"I think you like him."

At her words, I squeezed my eyes shut. "Not helping."

"I'm sorry. But you know, it's okay to have feelings for him. The world won't end if you do."

"He has feelings for me. He's hurt that I don't feel the same way," I argued. "The situation isn't about what I want. It's never been about what I want. He's never asked what I wanted, or—"

"What *do* you want, Tori?"

Her question silenced me.

"He hasn't asked, but I am. If you could do anything today, or tomorrow, or next week, what would you do?"

I forced myself to think about it.

To picture what tomorrow would look like, if I could do anything I wanted.

I closed my eyes, and saw myself at the theme park.

Not alone—I didn't like doing things alone.

I tried to picture myself there with Sienna, but it didn't feel honest. It didn't feel honest to imagine being there with Love, or any of the other women from the pack. Or any of the men from the pack, either.

When I saw myself there with Ronin, it felt right.

That was what I wanted.

I forced myself to consider the next week.

When we were back from our vacation, I saw myself going to work...

Then going home.

To Ronin's house.

When I tried to picture going back to the place I'd shared with Sienna, it made me nauseous.

"Shit," I whispered into the phone, my eyes still closed. "I want him... but I still don't want a mate."

"Do you not want a mate, or are you just not ready to commit to him yet?"

The words hit me hard.

I slouched lower. "I don't know."

"Just think about it. You know we love you, and we're here for you, no matter what you think or how you feel."

"I know." My words were soft, but honest. "I love you too. Bye."

We hung up, and I set my phone down on the coffee table in front of my couch.

We always had each other's backs, no matter what.

That would never change, regardless of what happened.

But my feelings... well, they scared me.

And I still felt hurt by what Ronin had said. More accurately, by the way he hadn't believed me.

Someone dropped off my sugary, alcoholic drink, some unappetizing butter cookies with a bit of jam on them, and my cheese fries.

I made it through half the glass and a third of the fries before it occurred to me that I didn't have my bag.

Which meant I didn't have any money.

Shit.

I glanced at my room key.

The next time the server came over, I'd ask them if that would work. If not, I'd be forced to call Ronin for help.

Which would positively suck.

Hopefully, the card would suffice.

I ate my way through the rest of the fries, and finished off the drink too. I nibbled at the jam cookies, which tasted slightly better than they looked.

When the server came back and asked if I wanted another drink, I chickened out and didn't ask about my room key.

Instead, I ordered two more drinks and another plate of cheese fries.
And some sliders.

Hopefully the alcohol would calm me down enough that I wasn't so hurt... or so violently against talking to Ronin again.

Before they came back with my food, a man I didn't recognize entered the bar.

He was too tall to be human, and not inked-up enough to be a shifter. Some of us didn't have tattoos, but almost all of us did.

That meant he was most-likely either a demon, fae, or vampire.

I prayed he was one of the first.

But of course, his nostrils flared immediately upon entering the room, and his gaze snapped toward me.

Vampire.

His warm eyes moved down my body, and I saw the satisfaction in them. My scent made me smell like the perfect meal, and my messy appearance made me look like the perfect target.

Neither of which bode well for me.

As expected, he crossed the room in a few long, lazy steps.

And sat down right beside me on the couch.

"Enjoying the beach, Beautiful?" he all but purred.

"Apparently." I gestured to myself, trying to decide what the best move was in my current situation.

Calling Ronin was obviously unnecessary. We were in public, so the vampire wouldn't attack me. He would try to seduce me, first.

My best bet would be to try proving to him that I wasn't someone he could talk into his bed, or into being his meal.

He chuckled, sliding a hand through his artfully-styled hair. "I could use some of that enjoyment in my life. Can I buy you another drink?"

I smiled, forcing my fangs to descend so he would see that I was a vampire too. "My mate would have a problem with that."

The interest in his gaze only thickened. "I don't see a mate."

"Even supernaturals have to use the bathroom every now and then. I'd expect you to know that, given what you are." I gestured to him.

He flashed me a wicked grin. "And what are you? Your scent tells me you're either mine, or something far more enticing."

Shit on a cracker.

"I—" I started to throw some bullshit together, but was saved by the ringing of my phone.

Ronin's name was on the screen.

"Sorry, that would be my mate." I gave the vampire another smile and lifted the phone to my ear. "Hey, Alpha."

# thirteen

## RONIN

"HEY, ALPHA." Tori's words were playful, but her voice wasn't.

Something was wrong.

"Where are you?" I growled into the phone, my heart beating hard in my chest.

It hadn't taken me long to regret asking my mate to leave me alone.

Knowing she was in the other room, likely frustrated with me, made me feel like shit.

But I forced myself to stay in the shower until I was sure my anger was gone, and I felt calmer about the fact that I cared about her more than she cared about me.

Winning her heart was a process.

I had to remember that.

And stepping into the room and finding her gone?

It scared the hell out of me.

She laughed.

The sound was forced.

"Our drinks will be out any second. See you soon."

With that, she hung up on me.

What the hell was going on?

I yanked jeans up my thighs and buttoned them as I stormed out of the room, only bothering to grab my phone so I could call her again if I didn't find her in the hotel's bar. Something was obviously up, but her words seemed to point me there.

I hit the elevator button, but when it didn't start rising immediately, I abandoned it and jogged to the stairs.

Taking them three at a time, I reached the bottom soon enough, and was in the bar a moment later.

When I found another man sitting on the couch next to my female, I barely suppressed a snarl.

The relief in her eyes when she saw me walking toward her kept me from losing my shit altogether.

She stood as I approached, and tucked herself under my arm, snuggling in close. "Hey, Handsome."

"What the fuck is going on?" My glare was pointed at the other man.

He stood too, clearing his throat. "There was a misunder-standing," he began. "I actually have to go. It was nice meeting you... what did you say your name was?"

"Tori Vex." Her smile was bright, but her gaze was sharp.

Though I knew she was only using my last name to protect herself, I couldn't prevent the surge of pride I felt at hearing it on her lips.

*Tori Vex.*

I'd be hearing it on replay in my mind in every spare minute.

His gaze jerked toward me, and I saw as realization dawned in his eyes.

He dipped his head in a rough nod, and all but fled the bar.

When he was gone, I looked at Tori.

She spoke before I could. "Before you flip out, I would like it to be known that I did not start a conversation with him, or invite him to sit next to me. He's a vampire. He caught my scent as soon as he came in here, and he made himself at home on my couch. I just came down here to give you space."

I let out a long breath.

Her expression was defiant, but her gaze was... worried.

Did she think I wasn't going to believe her?

I guided her back down to the couch so she would realize I wasn't going to lose my temper. "What did he say?"

"Nothing, really. He was just trying to seduce me into feeding him. I told him I had a mate, and he questioned whether or not you were real."

My nostrils flared. "You should've called me."

"You wanted to be alone."

I clenched my jaw.

A server arrived with two drinks, a plate of fries, and small platter of sliders.

I waited until the server was gone before growling, "He bought you food and a drink?"

"No. I bought myself food, and two drinks. Technically three. He was only here for a few minutes." She lifted one of the drinks, and took a long, slow sip of it.

I watched her tongue as it skated out and dragged over the rim of the glass, licking away what had to be either sugar or salt.

I wanted to taste it on her lips, but forced myself to ignore the urge.

The last time I'd kissed her in public, it hadn't gone well.

"Tori Vex?" I asked, when I managed to pull my gaze away from her mouth.

"We *are* mates, aren't we? I can't imagine you're going to let me go without changing my name at this point." She plucked a fry off the tray, picking the one covered in the most cheese and bacon bits. "Despite how much you wish you'd ended up with someone softer and sweeter."

I blinked.

She took a bite of her fry.

Had she just suggested I wanted someone other than her?

She had, hadn't she?

My eyes narrowed.

She popped the rest of the fry in her mouth.

I strode across the room, leaning over the countertop. The human at the register shrank away from me, obviously intimidated by my size. "Has the redhead on the couch paid yet?"

The human looked nervously at their screen. "No..."

"Charge it to room seven-twelve. Ronin Vex. Add whatever the fee is, and send it all up on a cart with two steaks and a handful of sides. I don't care what it costs."

The human nodded quickly. "Of course."

"Throw in a tip for whoever served her and yourself, too. Thirty percent."

Their eyes lit up. "Thank you."

I ignored the gratitude and walked back to the couch, where Tori was still having her way with the fries.

Without another word, I grabbed her by the waist and threw her over my shoulder. Rather than shrieking, she huffed at me. "I was eating, Ronin."

"You'll eat in our room."

I took a few steps, and noticed she was wearing my shirt.

It was sliding down toward her stomach, leaving her thong —and most of her sexy little ass—on display for the rest of the world to see.

Muttering a curse, I tugged the fabric back over her backside and headed for the stairs.

That ass was mine.

# fourteen

## TORI

I SHOULD'VE STAYED in the hotel room.

If I'd known that leaving would lead to me getting hit on by a hungry vampire, then carried ass-first back to the room anyway, I wouldn't have bothered going.

Then again, the fries had been *really* good.

And I was pretty sure Ronin had paid for everything when he went to the front of the bar, so that was also good. I hadn't been looking forward to the awkward moment when I had to tell the server that I didn't have money with me.

But still.

Staying would've been the better call.

Ronin slammed the door behind us, then set me down on the bed. My landing wasn't gentle, but it wasn't painful either. I always liked how rough he was.

"We need to talk," he said.

"Well, that sounds ominous." I tried to run a hand through my hair, and made a face when my fingers caught in the salty tangles. It felt a bit crunchy, which was never appealing. "I told you, I did not encourage that guy. I would've made something up if I didn't want you to find me down there with him. Instead, I told you where I was without letting him know I—"

"Not about the vampire." He growled the words... then slowly kneeled between my legs, so we were almost face to face. He was actually a bit lower than me thanks to the height of the bed. Seeing him beneath me gave me a bit of a power rush, though logically I knew he could still rip me apart if he wanted to.

His hands landed lightly on my knees. "I'm sorry, Tor."

I blinked again.

Had he just apologized?

I must've heard wrong.

"You're *what*?" The question slipped out before I could reconsider. By the time I regretted asking, it was too late to take it back.

"I'm *sorry*." He emphasized the apology, leaving no doubt about what he was saying. "What happened on the beach scared me. I didn't react well. I shouldn't have pushed you away in the shower, or brought up what I did. I'm sorry."

That was... actually a decent apology.

But I still felt self-conscious about what he'd said. About the way he hadn't believed me—especially about him thinking I would've accepted any guy's random invitation if it meant going on a vacation. That was hurtful.

I hadn't been opening up to him or trying to intensify our relationship, but I also hadn't flirted with anyone else. Or otherwise even considered cheating on him.

I hadn't wanted to be his mate, but that didn't mean I genuinely disbelieved that we were mates, or actively worked against it.

"I get it. It's easy to lash out when emotions get the best of you." I patted him on the hand.

His forehead wrinkled.

"I think I'm going to take my turn in the shower." My voice was light, though I didn't feel an ounce of the happiness I was feigning.

I was just... confused.

Overwhelmed, too.

Uncertain?

Definitelyyy.

And what was I supposed to do about it? Talk to him? Tell him he hurt me?

That sounded like a good way to hurt him too, and to accomplish nothing else in the process.

The wrinkles in his forehead deepened, but he let me go.

I slipped into the bathroom and locked the door behind me. Letting out a long breath, I crossed the room and turned on the shower, then stepped out to let it warm up.

As I peeled Ronin's shirt over my head, I heard something.

Something like... footsteps?

Frowning, I padded back to the door and pressed my ear to it.

Definitely footsteps.

They walked away from me, then back toward me.

Away, and back.

Away, and back.

Away, and back.

He was pacing.

*"You didn't really accept his apology,"* my wolf murmured. *"I'm sure he can tell something's wrong. He's not daft."*

*"I don't want to talk about it, though,"* I said.

*"He probably realizes that too."*

I sighed inwardly, then stepped back and took off my swimsuit.

Just before I stepped into the shower, his fist rapped against the door. "Tori?"

Dammit.

"Yeah?" I tried to make my voice sound cheerful.

"Can I..." he trailed off before clearing his throat and calling out, "Is there room for two in there?"

He was using my own question against me.

Clever, clever asshole.

If I turned him down, he would know something was wrong. If I didn't, he would probably want to talk more, and I really didn't want to talk.

But if I let him in, I *also* might be able to make him believe I was fine.

The chance of convincing him all was well was enough for me. "Sure, give me a second." I stepped under the shower long enough to make sure I was fully soaked, then stepped out and opened the door for him.

I expected his gaze to travel right down my body.

Instead, it landed on my face, and stayed.

Dammit, he was going to realize I was upset.

I should've turned him down.

It was too late for that, so I made my way back to the shower.

Rather than taking his pants off and joining me, he leaned up against the sink and watched as I got back in.

"I thought you wanted to shower with me." My voice was as playful as I could possibly force it to get.

"First, I want to talk. You're obviously upset."

I let out a long breath. "I didn't let you in to talk, Ronin. I'm fine."

"Don't lie to me," he warned. "This is important, Tor. I want to know why you're mad."

"I'm not mad," I shot back.

"Just tell me."

"Your Alpha shit isn't going to work on me, Ronin."

I heard him unzip his pants, and a moment later, his chest was against my back.

I couldn't stop my sharp inhale when his erection met my spine and his hands slid over my abdomen and breasts.

My back arched, and his hands continued moving slowly.

"I hate knowing I've upset you. Please just tell me. I want the truth, even if it's shitty."

I closed my eyes, leaning the back of my head against his shoulder. "It's been a long day. Let's just figure it out tomorrow."

He made a noise of disagreement. "Let's figure it out now, so I can make love to you in this shower, then eat you out while you feast on—"

There was a knock on our room's door, and someone called out something muffled that sounded like, "Room service!"

"Leave it in the bedroom," Ronin called back, his voice booming.

I heard the door click open, and a minute later, heard it shut again.

He stayed where he was, waiting until he was certain the person had left the room before his attention returned to me. "What was I saying?"

"You were going to eat me out while I feasted on..." I drawled.

"Cheese fries," he clarified. "And steak. I ordered steak."

Yumm.

"Tell me what's wrong so we can deal with it and move on to that part of the night," he said, his hands resuming their slow, sensual movements over my body.

"I don't want to."

"I'll have to assume the worst, then."

"What's the worst?"

"You're madly in love with the vampire you met earlier, so I have to hunt him down and slit his throat," he said, matter-of-factly.

I snorted. "Yeah, right."

"It's the only logical reason why you won't just tell me."

I shook my head. "It doesn't matter."

"It does to me."

"You just can't let it go, can you?"

"Not when it comes to you." He dragged his palm over my hip bone and let his fingers move lightly over it, testing and feeling. It made me wet, though the shower thankfully hid that.

I huffed. "Fine, Ronin. You want the truth? It hurt me when you didn't believe that I wanted to be here with *you*. When you said I'd just as easily be here with any other man in the pack."

His body went still.

His hands did, too.

The floodgates were open, so more words spewed out. "Before I met you, that was absolutely true, but I've been loyal since we've been together. I shut guys down when they try to flirt with me. I don't check people out. If someone propositioned me with a vacation, I would tell them I had a mate. You made it clear you don't believe that, you don't believe in me, and it makes me feel like shit."

He didn't respond immediately.

I couldn't help but fill the silence. "Yes, I didn't want a mate when we first met. I still don't feel ready to commit myself to you, either. But I'm here, aren't I? I'm trying. I've *been* trying. Maybe not to be everything you ever hoped and dreamed for, but to be enough to satisfy you and keep you company without taking away my freedom entirely."

I added, "I get that you've been lonely for longer than I can imagine, okay? I get it. But I've been trapped for most of my life. I've been used, and hurt, and drained, like I'm an object.

I just want to live, Ronin. I just want to see things, go on adventures, and experience life. I didn't want a mate because I wanted my freedom—and I'm sorry that's ruining your life. But I can't change that. I can't wipe away who I am for you. And I don't want to."

"I don't want that either, Tori." His voice was low. "I've never wanted you to change. I want to make you happy."

"And to make me yours."

"Of course. That's in my veins. But you'll be a hell of a lot freer, and safer, when you're mine. We can go anywhere— we can do anything. I don't give a damn where I am, as long as you're there too."

"I'm starting to realize that, but it's not something I can wrap my mind around overnight."

"You have all the time you need, Tor."

"I don't think I do. You made it clear today that what I can offer right now isn't enough for you."

He scoffed. "Like hell it isn't."

"You're not happy, Ronin."

"I wasn't happy after what happened on the beach, but overall, I'm happier having you around. Even when you're avoiding me. I'm sorry I made you feel like you weren't enough for me—it won't happen again."

"I don't know."

"Let me prove it to you. The rest of the vacation will be a fucking dream."

"I'm tired, Ronin."

"I can fix that too. Dinner will help. Letting me taste you will too."

My body warmed. "I didn't agree to that yet."

"*Yet*, being the key word."

My lips curved upward. "No one's ever gone down on me before."

"I know. I haven't stopped thinking about that since you told me earlier. I would've had you on my tongue on the beach if that bastard hadn't interrupted us."

A laugh escaped me. "No wonder you were such a grump."

He chuckled, his chest rumbling against my back. "Let's get you washed up so I can feed you and have my way with you."

"No protests here."

Ronin eased my body away from his, then stepped around to the front of me. His hands caught my face, and he tilted my head as he leaned down.

His lips met mine, and the kiss was soft.

Slow.
Soul-achingly sweet.

Our tongues moved together, the dance unlike anything I'd ever experienced before.

Vulnerable.

Intimate.

When he pulled away, I was dizzy from the gentle intensity of it.

"Wash your hair while I enjoy your body," he murmured to me, stepping behind me again and letting his hands slide over my torso once more.

"Yes, Alpha," I teased, but there was no bite to it.

He touched me while I washed up, not to get me worked up but just to feel me. I had never felt so desirable—or so important to someone.

I could definitely get used to feeling like that.

When we got out of the shower, Ronin helped me into a robe, but didn't bother with one of his own. I teased him when he put a pair of boxer briefs on, but the sight was incredible.

We ate together in peace, still sitting across from each other on the bed, and it was even more comfortable than our last meal had been.

When the food was gone, I was so far from horny, it was ridiculous.

"How do you feel about watching a movie before we get on with tonight's planned activities?" I asked. "I'm too full for... what we were talking about."

"That sounds nice." He pulled the blankets on his bed back, making space for both of us before he lowered himself to his side and patted the bed next to him.

I didn't hesitate to slip under the blankets.

He pulled my back to his chest, and handed me the remote. While I turned on a chick-flick I'd seen a few times, his hand skimmed over my hip, on top of the robe I still had on.

"What are you doing?" I murmured, as the movie started.

"Whatever I want with you." He nipped lightly at my neck, and my lips curved upward.

His hands kept moving over my robe, sliding over my breasts, abdomen, and core.

As the movie's love interests ran into each other—literally—he finally untied my robe.

I sucked in a breath as his warm fingers brushed my breast. They circled my nipples one by one, and my entire body warmed.

His hand finally slid down my abdomen, and to my core. I couldn't stop my gasp when he found my folds, and slipped over my clit.

"You're so fucking sexy," he said against my ear. His free hand caught my robe, pulling the back of it up higher as he leaned in. His erection, covered only by the thin fabric of his boxer-briefs, nestled against my ass cheeks.

He continued stroking my clit, working me slowly. Though my desire grew intense, Ronin wasn't in a hurry. The movie played in the background, and though my eyes were on it, I was lost in the rush of his touch.

Eventually, his fingers left me.

Before I had a chance to complain, his head was under the blankets, his face between my thighs.

I cried out at the sensation.

At his tongue tracing me, flicking me.

At his fingers opening me and filling me while he dragged me to the edge so insanely fast with his mouth.

I shattered on him, and he worked me harder.

Faster.

Ronin got me off again, and again, and again.

"I need you," I breathed, when his fingers and mouth weren't enough for me anymore.

"Not yet." He nipped at my clit with his teeth, making my hips jerk.

"*Now*, Ronin."

"Yes, Alpha." His sexy drawl made me laugh breathlessly.

He lifted himself over the top of me, his massive body pressing my back into the mattress.

I moaned when he rubbed the head of his cock over my clit and slit.

I groaned when he rocked lightly against my entrance.

And I cried out when he finally slid inside me.

It was bliss.

He was bliss.

*We* were bliss.

...Maybe I wanted a mate after all.


The TV was dark and the hotel was quiet when we finally collapsed in each other's arms, spent and sticky.

"Want me to go to the other bed?" Ronin mumbled.

His arms were heavy in the best way, his body warm too.

"Not tonight." My words were muffled, but I didn't even consider letting him go.

"Good. You belong here."

My lips curved upward as I drifted off.

# fifteen

## TORI

The rest of the week passed by in a blur of fun and exhaustion.

With a side of sex, of course.

It wasn't the focus, though.

We spent five days exploring the different parts of the theme park, arriving before it opened and leaving when they kicked us out every single day.

We rode every ride, at least twice each. Even the kid ones. I lost count of how many times we went on the best ones.

We bought at least one of every unique snack or treat we passed.

We danced when music played.

We oohed, ahhed, and laughed at the terrible jokes in the stupid shows the workers put on.

We wore the cute accessories the gift shops sold. Ronin did that with reluctance, though I did it with enthusiasm.

We took a hundred pictures together, and even more just of each other.

It was the most fun I had *ever* had.

And as the days went by, I began having a very, very hard time picturing a future for myself that didn't include Ronin Vex.

We slept in until nearly noon the day we were heading home. Ronin picked a late flight for the sake of catching up on sleep, and so we could stop at the beach one more time before we headed out.

After we were up, we packed our bags and made our way down to the hotel's restaurant. We had a long, relaxed lunch, then left our bags at the front desk and walked to the beach.

We were both quiet as we set up two lounge chairs beside each other. He captured my hand and laced his fingers through mine, sliding over until our sides met.

We watched the waves crash, both of us quiet. My mind moved over the past few days, and my lips curved upward as I remembered bits and pieces of everything we'd seen and done.

His thumb dragged rhythmically over my knuckle, the touch light and comforting.

"Thank you," I finally said, breaking the silence after some time had passed.

"For what?" His thumb continued moving, with absolutely no rush to it.

"Bringing me here. I wanted to have experiences like this, and had no way of making them happen. This was... perfect."

He lifted our intertwined hands to his mouth and kissed the top of my knuckles. "This is only the beginning, Tor. We have the rest of eternity."

I nodded, though I bit my lip when I looked back out at the ocean.

Eternity was terrifying.

The honeymoon phase was going to end when we got back to Wildwood, and we'd have to figure out how to live together with our new dynamics.

It wasn't going to be easy.

I wished we could just stay on vacation forever.

It wasn't reasonable... but it sure as hell sounded good.

We remained where we were until it was time to go, then we hopped in our rental car and headed back to the airport.

Back to Wildwood.

And back to reality.

Things remained at our new normal, up until we pulled into Ronin's driveway and found a giant of a man leaning up against the garage door. He had light brown skin and tight, dark curls.

My forehead wrinkled. "Who's that?"

Ronin's eyes were narrowed. "Vander, my beta. He doesn't make a habit of hanging out in front of my house. Stay in the truck while I figure out what's going on."

When he opened his door, I gave it about thirty seconds before I opened mine.

"What's the problem?" Ronin cut straight to it, not bothering with any bullshit. He flashed me a warning look when I closed the passenger door behind me, but I ignored it.

"A vampire was spotted near the town's border a few days ago. We assume they're looking for the blood wolves. I have our pack patrolling with the Wildwood enforcers for now."

"Why wasn't I informed?" Ronin's voice was low, his anger barely suppressed.

"You needed time with your mate. Hello, by the way." Vander dipped his head toward me before refocusing on Ronin. "Madd and Love offered you a house in the middle of their pack's neighborhood for the time being."

"Fine." Ronin's reply was short and clipped.

"Was anyone hurt?" I asked, stepping up to the front of the truck.

"No. We've still only seen the one vampire. You're safe."

Ronin's nostrils flared.

If we'd been on vacation, I would've taken his hand just to calm him down a little. Because we weren't, I wasn't sure what to do.

Touch him?

Give him space?

I had no idea.

"Thanks for letting us know," I said, wrapping my arms over my stomach so I didn't do something less logical with them. "We'll make our way to Madd's land soon."

Vander dipped his head, then strode around the back of the house, heading straight into the forest. There was no fence to keep him out of our yard, and even if there was, he would've used it if he was really Ronin's beta.

My mate's hand was on my lower back, propelling me into the house, the moment his beta disappeared. He unlocked the door with my back tucked up against his chest, and locked it behind us immediately.

By the time he stepped away from me, his phone was already against his ear, his expression murderous.

"What the fuck were you thinking?" he snarled into the phone, stalking toward our bedroom. "Of all people, you should know better than to keep this shit from me, Madd." He had another duffel bag free from the closet in seconds, and tossed toiletries in it rapidly.

I watched in silence as he argued with Madd, and packed more shit. Some of mine, and some of his. When the work shirts I rarely bothered wearing to work went in the bag, I realized exactly what was going on.

Ronin was *panicking*.

He knew I was in danger, and it was scaring him.

But what was I supposed to do about it?

I would always be in danger. Always.

My safety could never be a guarantee.

I was a blood wolf. Vampires would always want to use me as a living blood bag, and there was no escaping that.

A sealed mate bond could ensure that Ronin and I were a packaged deal, but who was to say that some vampires wouldn't eventually try to take both of us?

Me, for my blood, and him, to keep me alive?

If he couldn't handle me being at risk, an *eternal mate bond* was a pipe dream.

I was quiet while he packed for us, and when he remained on his phone with Madd through the drive to the pack's neighborhood.

Ronin paused his call long enough to carry our bags into the house we'd been offered, then kissed me goodbye and strode out, warning me to stay put.

My gaze moved over the neutral-colored furniture and the calm décor.

It was pretty, but I would've much rather been in Ronin's house.

*Our* house.

I ran my fingers through my curls, then pulled my phone from my pocket and texted my friends.

ME

**Where are you guys?**

LOVE

On house arrest at my place

Sienna made about a thousand sugar cookies

SIENNA

*three hundred*

LOVE

I'll count them to settle this

ME

**I'm headed over to you**

SIENNA

Are you mad at us from keeping the vamp
sighting a secret?

ME

Nah, just grateful

LOVE

We knew Ronin would have you on a plane
back here in a heartbeat

ME

I'm glad you didn't tell him

It was so damn much fun

They both liked my message, and I slipped out of the house. Ronin would be pissed—and panicky—if he got home before me, so I'd try to be back before him.

Probably.

But I didn't appreciate the way he'd abandoned me. Or the way he hadn't asked for my opinion before leaving. Even if he was the expert in the situation, he should've asked what I wanted, or at least made sure I was comfortable with his plan.

So, maybe I wouldn't try.

That was a decision for my future self to figure out.

I left the house, passing a few of the pack ladies I was friendly with on the way to Love's place. More people were out and about than usual, which seemed like either a good sign or a bad one. Or a bit of both.

Bauther was sitting on a chair on the porch, obviously keeping watch over the house (and the women in it) when I arrived. He gave me a nod of greeting.

"You on babysitting duty?" I teased him, as I walked up the porch steps.

"Something like that." His voice was low and rumbly, but it did nothing for me. After being with Ronin, I didn't see how anyone else's possibly could.

"Have fun," I called over my shoulder, as I knocked on Love's door before walking right in.

On a normal day, I wouldn't dare walk in without waiting for someone to answer. Who knew what freaky shit the two of them could be up to. But considering Sienna was there, and they were on house arrest, it seemed fairly safe.

"Hey!" Sienna smiled when she saw me. There was a sugar cookie in one of her hands, and a tube of icing in the other. The cookies were shaped like paw prints, and she was decorating them in fun colors that didn't resemble actual paw prints in the slightest.

I loved them.

Love was sitting on a barstool at her kitchen's island, and immediately slipped off of it when she saw me. She threw her arms around me, and I hugged her back tightly, emotion suddenly swelling in my throat.

"You guys weren't in actual danger, were you?" I asked.

Love scoffed. "Of course not. The vampire got into *Coffee, Toffee, & Cake* while me and Sienna were working, but Madd always has at least one wolf sitting at a table in the front area. The vamp reacted slightly to one of our scents, and the wolf escorted him out of town. Neither of us even realized anything had happened until my mate showed up and dragged us back here."

"How long ago was that?" I checked.

"It's been three days," Sienna said.

My eyebrows shot upward. "Has Madd been back?"

"He's in and out. Never stays for long. He's trying to keep himself from losing his shit," Love explained. "We haven't been alone since before the vampire showed up, so I'm sure he's going to reach the end of his patience soon. He misses me."

The easy way she said that made my throat constrict.

*He misses me.*

What would it feel like to know that Ronin missed me when we were apart? Not that he was worried about me, or that he wanted to touch me, but that he *missed* me. Missed my personality, missed my smile, missed *me.*

I had no idea, but it sounded good.

Hell, it even *felt* good.

And honestly?

I already missed him. The version of him I'd had on vacation, at least. The version of him that joked around, had fun, and laughed with me. The version that always wanted me, no matter where we were or what else could happen.

But if he didn't miss me, it didn't really matter, did it?

"What happens when he's at the end of his patience?" I asked, taking the stool beside Love's as we sat back down.

"He'll leave the patrols to the enforcers, like he should've in the beginning. Between your pack and mine, we have way more than enough man-power to keep an eye on the town. And all they really need is for someone to follow us when we leave; it's not like the vampires are here for Sienna's cookies."

"Though they should be," she said, pointing a finger-gun at Love.

"They should," I agreed, reaching over and taking a cookie. "All of these cookies match, so I'm assuming there's an occasion."

"Isa's baby shower is today," Sienna explained. "One of her friends offered to pay me. I tried to decline the money, but they insisted."

"She already has three more baby showers on the books now, and two bridal showers," Love added, her eyes bright as she stole my cookie and took a bite. "If she keeps going at this rate, she'll be leaving us alone at the bakery sooner rather than later. And there are three-hundred fifty-nine cookies, by the way. I counted."

"They ordered three hundred. The pack is huge, so there are fifty extra, and a handful more just in case I mess up."

I stole my cookie back from Love and bit into it, sighing at the delicious flavor. "Oh, I missed this."

"You had a lot more fun on your trip than you would've here," Love said. "Tell us about it."

"Was that an order?" I teased.

"Nah, alphas can't order each other around." She winked at me.

I rolled my eyes. "I'm not an alpha."

Love patted my hand. "Honey, you're mated to Ronin. That makes you the alpha female of your pack."

"Technically, their bond isn't sealed," Sienna pointed out. "Is it?"

"*Hell* no."

Sienna snorted.

Love rolled her eyes. "Don't be dramatic. Mating is fun, as I'm sure you experienced this past week."

My face warmed at her reminder, and images flashed through my mind. Memories of us laughing together, teasing each other, in bed together...

"We were honeymooning. I knew everything would change as soon as we got back," I finally said. "I just didn't expect it to change like this. He didn't ask my opinion about anything—just made up his mind and stormed out of the house."

"Male werewolves will control everything if you let them," Love agreed. "The alphas, at least. You have to decide what you're willing to compromise on and stand up for yourself. Madd wanted me to stay glued to his side until the vampires were dealt with, but I refused, so we agreed that me staying here with a guard dog was acceptable."

"How did you get him to pause long enough to have that conversation?" I wondered.

"I dragged him to the bathtub."

I blinked.

Sienna did too.

"We take baths together. It's a thing." She shrugged. "Both of us are trapped when we're in the tub together. And the nudity is fun. Baths force us to talk about things instead of charging ahead."

I guess if it worked, that was what mattered.

"How is Bauther, by the way?" Love asked me.

"He's fine. Could probably use a cookie," I said absent-mindedly.

"Everyone could use a cookie," Sienna tossed back.

"Definitely. You should bring him one." Love wagged her eyebrows at Sienna, and Sienna blushed.

My eyes widened. "Is something going on between you?"

"No." Sienna's voice was firm. "Love wants there to be, but there's not. He just stares at me a lot. It's unnerving."

"Sexy unnerving, or creepy unnerving?"

"Creepy," she said too quickly.

"Liar." Love reached over and snagged a cookie off the tray. "I'm going to give him this and ask if he's interested in *your* cookie."

Sienna groaned.

I snorted.

"Casual sex can be fun," I pointed out. "If you're still wearing the perfume, it should conceal your scent enough to give it a try."

"We are not discussing this." Sienna plucked the cookie from Love's hand. "And I'll give this to him myself, *without* the suggestive comment."

"Everyone needs a little more suggestiveness in their life," Love called over her shoulder.

"Except you," Sienna sang back.

I laughed, and Love grinned.

"You don't think they're mates, do you?" I asked.

"Nah. I see Sienna ending up with someone easy-going. Bauther's more laid-back than our alphas, but he'd lead the pack without batting an eye if he needed to. You know she's the only one of the three of us who could actually succeed at avoiding her soulmate for more than a few weeks."

"She'd be more polite about turning him down than we are," I agreed. "He wouldn't know what to do."

"Unless he's as calm about it as she is."

"Which Bauther couldn't be?" I checked.

I didn't know him well, but I'd talked to him a few times. He seemed pretty relaxed to me.

"Nope." Love stole my cookie and took another bite.

The front door shut as Sienna strode back into the kitchen, huffing at us. "I told you he would stare at me."

"You can't fault him for being smart enough not to look away from a beautiful woman," Love teased.

Sienna scowled, and I couldn't bite back another laugh.

As much fun as I'd had on vacation with Ronin, it was damn good to be home.

Even if home was a little up in the air at the moment.

# *sixteen*

## TORI

WE WENT to the baby shower, and were walking back to Love's house when my phone rang. I didn't even have to look at the screen to know who was calling me.

The other girls flashed me knowing looks and stepped inside the house, and I stayed out on the porch. Bauther was behind me, heading right back to the rocking chair he'd occupied earlier.

"Hello?" I said into the phone, like my heartbeat hadn't picked up in anticipation of a lecture.

"Where the fuck are you?" Ronin's snarl was exactly what I had expected, word for word. "You said you would stay home."

"*You* said I would stay at the house we've been temporarily loaned," I corrected. "I'm not a dog you can command to *stay*."

"Where are you?"

"I've been with Love and Sienna since you abandoned me. We were at Love's place until two hours ago, then at a baby shower, and now we're back at Love's."

There was a tense moment of silence.

I added, "If it makes you feel any better, Bauther has been babysitting us all day."

"It doesn't make me feel better to know that another man has had his eyes on you all day when I thought you were home," he growled.

"Maybe you should've taken a few minutes to ask me politely whether I was willing to spend all day in a strange house with absolutely nothing to do, then."

He let out a harsh breath. "I need to see you."

"You know where to find me. And if you show up here, you'd better not be growling at me when you do."

"Are you telling me to change my attitude, Tor?" The frustration in his voice had an edge to it. It was almost... playful.

Like it had been on vacation, but with a lot more stress behind it.

"Yup. Assuming you can handle it, I'll see you soon."

"You will, Alpha."

I bit my lip to hide my smile, and hung up the phone.

My phone vibrated a fraction of a second later.

RONIN

I'd like to hear a bye before you hang up
on me

ME

Then maybe you should give me the same
courtesy before you order me to stay put
and leave

RONIN

I kissed you

That's almost the same

ME

And me saying I'd see you soon was
almost the same as goodbye

RONIN

I feel like you're winning this argument

ME

If you want to be my mate, you're going to
have to get used to that

RONIN

Don't make me hard when I'm walking in
another pack's neighborhood

ME

LOL

I tucked my phone in my pocket, and finally turned back toward the door. My gaze caught on Bauther's, and his expression was knowing.

"Don't take a mate," I told him, messing with my hair a bit more. "It just makes everything more complicated."

He chuckled. "The end result is worth the growing pains."

I liked that take on it.

*Growing pains.*

It was much more romantic to think of them that way instead of as disagreements or shitty communication.

And didn't big changes always come with growing pains?

It had been a struggle to figure out life right after Love and I got away from the clan. A few times, I'd even wondered if we would be better off going back to them, where we knew we would at least have enough food to eat.

The struggle had been worth it a million times over. I'd suffer again in a heartbeat for my freedom.

And I had never regretted deciding to stay in Wildwood. Not even after Ronin abducted me from the bakery.

Which was... something to think about, I guess.

But yeah.

Growing pains.

I liked that.

I helped Love and Sienna clean up the cookie mess in the kitchen for a minute, before Love's phone rang.

The way her eyes lit up told me who was calling her.

I heard her playful, "Hey, Archie," as she ducked into the other room, and it made my lips curve upward.

"You look happier," Sienna said, as I wiped hardened bits of icing off the countertop and into my palm. It was more transportable than the trash bin.

"Happier than when?" I asked.

"When you were single." She flashed me a soft smile. "He makes you happy, doesn't he?"

"I'd like to say no." I walked over to the garbage, and dumped the frosting bits. "But I'd be lying. He pisses me off, he frustrates me, he drives me insane... but he does make me happy too."

"Good." She hip-bumped me on her way to the sink, and I grinned.

"Are you going to look for a mate now?"

"Not a chance. I have no desire to watch my world implode for a guy. I am thinking about getting a cat, though."

I laughed. "A *cat*?"

"Mmhm. They're low-maintenance, right?"

"I have no idea. I've never considered getting a cat."

"Well, I think I'm going to do it. Then I'll never be lonely enough to consider looking for a man."

There was a quick knock at the door, but there was no pause before it opened.

"That would be *your* man," Sienna teased me.
I rolled my eyes at her, but my smile didn't go anywhere.

Maybe I liked knowing he was mine.

Ronin was in the kitchen a heartbeat later, his intense gaze moving over my figure before he relaxed slightly, still striding toward me.

And damn, I'd managed to forget how big he was.

How pretty he was, too.

Those thick muscles, and that messy dark hair...

Yum.

He engulfed me in his arms, pulling me flush against his chest and squeezing tightly. Though he didn't say a word, he didn't really have to. I knew what he was feeling.

Relief.

Comfort.

Gratitude.

As much as it pained me to admit it, I understood why he was afraid of losing me. I really did. He had spent his life waiting to meet his mate, so it made sense that he was terrified of losing me.

I didn't blame him for that, even though I didn't appreciate the shitty way he'd expected me to do what he wanted earlier.

"I'm sorry I screwed up. Come home with me so we can figure it out," he murmured into my hair, his words soft enough that I didn't know whether Sienna would hear them.

And while the apology wasn't perfect, it was good enough for me.

"Alright," I agreed.

Love stepped back out of her room, her gaze knowing as it landed on me and Ronin. "You guys leaving?"

"Yep." I eased myself out of my mate's grasp, and he reluctantly let me go.

"Madd's headed home anyway. Finally decided he's had enough patrolling." Her smile was bright, and her eyes were even brighter.

"You called it," Sienna teased.

"Of course I did." She fluffed her hair. "I know him better than anyone."

Sienna laughed, and I smiled.

I wanted to know Ronin better than anyone, too.

"I'll take a detour and adopt a cat on the way home," Sienna said. "Maybe that'll get Bauther off my tail."

Love and I both snorted.

"The way he watches you, it's not likely," Love said. "I'm telling you, the man wants to become intimately acquainted with your body."

Sienna made a face. "I am *not* talking about this."

Ronin's arm slid around my waist and tugged me lightly toward the door.

As much as I liked being around my friends—really, they were more like my sisters—I knew I needed to talk to my mate.

So, I said my goodbyes, and we were off.

Part of me expected awkwardness between us as we walked back to the house we were staying at. We'd gotten in that little disagreement about the beach makeout situation in the hotel, but otherwise, we didn't really know how to disagree on things.

But, Ronin did away with that expectation when he laced his fingers through mine and walked at my side. Our arms brushed as we moved.

"Do you want to talk?" I asked him, as soon as we were far enough from the house that Bauther wouldn't hear us.

"Not until we're off the streets. I don't want Madd's pack knowing all of our shit."

It seemed like a good call to me.

There was no need to broadcast our *growing pains* to the whole neighborhood. What happened between us was between *us*.

So, we were quiet as we walked home. It wasn't awkward, like I'd expected it to be. It was just... quiet.

And maybe even a little bit calm.

Hopefully, we were ready to work through the problem and move on.

We reached the house soon enough. Ronin let me in first, closing and locking the door behind us.

I headed to the kitchen, deciding that if we were going to have a conversation, I wanted to cook dinner while we did so.

"There's no food here," Ronin said, as I started opening the fridge.

I paused.

Shit.

No cooking meant no distractions.

How was I supposed to have a conversation with him without any distractions?

Did we sit together at the kitchen table? Or climb into a borrowed bed that didn't smell anything like us before we talked?

Or...

I remembered what I'd asked Love.

It seemed so bizarre, but if it worked for them, why couldn't it work for us?

"Let's talk in the bathtub," I blurted. "We probably won't fit well, but—"

"We'll make it work." Ronin didn't bat an eye at what should've sounded like an insane idea. Maybe he was just glad I'd stopped being pissed about the way he abandoned me earlier.

Taking my hand again, he towed me to the master bedroom, then right into the bathroom. He had the water warming up a moment later, and his shirt went over his head.

My stress vanished for a minute as my eyes moved over his body.

Hot damn.

His jeans followed his shirt to the ground, and I was officially drooling.

"Are you getting in the tub in your clothes, Tor?" he asked.

Oh.

Right.

"No." I grabbed the hem of my bra, and had myself free of it quickly.

Ronin stepped out of his boxer-briefs while I took off my leggings and thong. Our gazes were on each other, though neither of us mentioned our growing desire. His was evident. Very, very evident.

He plugged the drain, then guided me to the tub with a hand on my lower back. Despite our horniness, neither of us made a move to instigate anything sexual.

There were shitty conversations to be had before that.

"You might need to get in first," I told him, looking around the tub. It wasn't tiny, but it wasn't gigantic either. And Ronin was huge. "I'll probably have to sit on you."

"Oh, the horror," he drawled.

I snorted, and he sat down, tugging me with him. We crashed into the tub with absolutely no smoothness whatsoever, and it knocked the breath right out of me.

I couldn't help but laugh as we got settled, my back to his chest and his erection raging against my ass. He chuckled too, his arms wrapping around me and squeezing lightly.

Maybe I could understand why Love was such a fan of shared baths.

# seventeen

## TORI

I LEANED the back of my head against Ronin's shoulder, and he ran his fingers slowly through my hair. The gesture felt nice, so I closed my eyes.

"I'm sorry I didn't ask what you wanted before leaving," he said, after a few minutes of blissful peace.

"It's okay. You were scared," I murmured.

"So fucking terrified." He squeezed me tighter with the arm still around me.

"I'm always going to be in danger, Ronin. I know it's not the best-case scenario for you. Your life would be better and easier if you were mated to a human woman. I—"

His grip on my hair tightened. Not painfully, but enough to cut me off.

His lips brushed my ear. "The next time you say my life would be better without you, I'm trapping you in the house for a week. No going outside. No working. No distractions. Just you and me, Tor."

"That would be torture," I grumbled.

Sure, the sex would be fun, but I'd get incredibly bored.

SO incredibly bored.

"Then stop trying to convince me to walk away from you," he said.

"I'm not trying to convince you to walk away. I'm just trying to get you to understand that my life isn't ever going to be simple. There will always be someone who wants a blood wolf. We're an easy source of food, and—"

"And when our bond is sealed, you'll be stuck with me as your only food source for life. They can't take you from me and still reap the benefits of you being a blood wolf. You'd die, and they would've wasted their time and money."

His words caught me off guard.

He'd said something similar before, but it hadn't really set in.

"I'm already addicted to you," I finally said.

"Which Madd and I believe the vampires already know," he confirmed. "The vampire you met in our hotel was part of a massive clan with many connections. I had my pack look into him after we met him."

I blinked.

That was... a lot.

But also a good call, if I was being honest.

"Then why didn't he try to take me?"

"He was probably going to, until he realized who you belong to. Taking my mate would immediately ignite a war. Not just between my pack and the vampire's clan, but between that clan and every wolf in our world. I have far too many connections for any vampire with a few brain cells to risk that kind of carnage. The supernatural community still hasn't come close to recovering from our war with the humans more than a century ago."

With his words, I relaxed a little.

Just a little, though.

"Then why do you think they sent someone here?"

"Madd and I were discussing that." He traced his fingers lightly over my hip, like he was debating telling me. "There's only one real conclusion."

"Spit it out, Ronin," I warned.

He was silent for another moment before he finally answered. "Sienna."

I blinked.

He continued dragging his fingers over my hip. "We need to get her mated if we want to keep the vampires out of Wildwood. And believe me, I know that's a hell of a lot easier said than done."

I was silent for a minute.

A long, long minute.

If mating would keep her safe, well, then I wanted her mated. As long as it was what she wanted.

Which I knew it wasn't.

"She doesn't want a mate," I finally said. "She's adopting a cat."

"A *cat*?" I heard the disdain in his voice.

We were wolves, after all. Which was pretty much the definition of *dog people*.

"Bauther and Smith from Madd's pack will take turns tailing her until we've found a mate for her. We're calling in unmated guys from around the world that we think might suit her."

I let out a long breath. "Please tell me you're joking."

"I'm not." He squeezed my hip lightly. "She's important to you. You're important to me. If keeping her safe means pairing her off with someone, we'll get it done."

"She covers her scent with perfume," I protested.

"So did you. It didn't stop me from recognizing you as mine the first moment I saw you."

I couldn't exactly argue.

I hadn't been able to look away from him either.

"She doesn't want a mate, Ronin. You need to respect that."

"I respect that she deserves to live free of vampires more than she deserves to live without a mate. And I respect that one of the men I've met over the past centuries may be searching for her desperately right now."

I groaned. "This conversation was *not* supposed to be about you playing matchmaker."

"You're right. It was about me apologizing for losing my shit, and promising I'd make it right. Part of the way I'll do that is by making sure your best friends are safe, permanently."

"I'm supposed to win our arguments, remember?" I tossed back.

"If the argument is about anything other than safety, it's yours."

I gave him a dramatic sigh. "I guess that's fair. But for the record, I *am* going to warn Sienna."

"I know you are." He kissed my cheek lightly. "Do you forgive me?"

"I don't see another option, since we're going to be stuck together forever."

He chuckled and squeezed my hip again. "That's the spirit."

"Mmhm." I relaxed against him, and he played with my hair lightly for a few minutes. Uncertainty set in slowly, and I found myself thinking aloud. "What does our life look like from here, Ronin?"

"We give things a few weeks to settle down. You start working again—a lot less than you were working before the vacation, because I know you were picking up extra shifts to stay away from me."

"Yeah, yeah."

He caught my earlobe between his teeth, and I shuddered at the light pull. "I'll get back to working on our house at a normal speed, so the damn thing actually gets done."

"I knew you were working slow on purpose," I grumbled, though my complaint was half-hearted.

He wanted me. It was hard to be angry at him for that.

"I was, and it worked." He tugged lightly on my ear again. "Our pack or Madd's will keep an eye on you whenever you're not with me. When things have settled down, we can go home again, with a beefier security system built in for my peace of mind. As soon as we're sure things are stable here, and you get the itch to leave, we can head out to one of the other places you've always wanted to go. I assume you have a list."

My heartbeat picked up.

Not in fear or anger, but in excitement. "I do."

"Good. We'll work through it whenever we get the chance. How does that sound?"

"Incredible." I turned my head, grabbing his face and pulling his mouth down to mine.

He kissed me slowly, lifting me off his lap long enough to turn me around. When he lowered me back down, the head of his cock pressed against my entrance.

I inhaled sharply.

He nipped at my bottom lip. "You going to let me do whatever I want with you, Tor?"

"Hell yes."

Ronin grinned, pulling me down over him just an inch. "I'm going to fill you with my pleasure and lick us both off your lips."

My body flushed. "Then what the hell are we doing in this tub?"

He laughed. "Good question."

With that, he stood and walked me out, sliding deeper into me with every step he took.

Instead of tossing me on the bed, or draping my back over the mattress, he pulled out of me as we reached the room.

I groaned when he did—but when he set me down on the bed facing away from him, I understood why he had.

My entire body pulsed with desire as he guided me onto my hands and knees, my ass in the air. I was insanely slick between my thighs, and not because of the bath.

Ronin's hands slid over my backside, spreading me open. "Fuck, this is the prettiest ass I've ever seen."

My body clenched. "Don't tease me. I want you now."

"Do you, Alpha?" He smacked my ass lightly. It wasn't a spank, but it made my body clench again. "Spread your legs for me, and I'll give you what you want."

I spread them.

Instead of giving me what I wanted, he dragged his fingers lightly over my clit. My body trembled, and I bit back a cry.

"You feel so damn good, Tor. Maybe I'll eat you before I get you on my cock."

I moaned, and he dragged my ass off the ledge of the bed, ducking and turning so he was positioned beneath me. He licked my clit once, and I cried out.

His chest rumbled, and his tongue got to work.

My cries grew more desperate, more frantic, as he dragged me to the edge with his mouth. His fingers parted me wider, filling my channel and toying with my ass as he licked and sucked.

When he finally dragged his teeth over me, it was over.

The sounds of my pleasure were so damn loud, my hips jerking and my body rocking with the release.

Ronin was rumbling again when I came down from the high —and as he slipped out from beneath me.

My body trembled with the loss of him, but he pinched my clit as he lifted me by the hips. In one smooth motion, he parted my legs wider and slid home.

My lips parted, my sounds dying with the feel of him entering me.

Filling me.

*Taking* me.

"Fuck, you were made for me." His words were silk, and my hips jerked in response. He slapped my ass again, still lightly. I tightened around him in response, sucking in a breath. "You like that, Tor?"

"Hell yes," I breathed.

I wanted more.

So did he.

He growled, and his palm hit my ass again, harder.

I cried out as pleasure rolled through me, and I shattered hard and fast. "Shit, Ronin!"

He snarled, slamming into me. We lost control together, and it was perfect.

Insanely perfect.

I collapsed on the bed, and he dropped down beside me, dragging me on top of his chest. He kissed my forehead, then my cheek, then my forehead again before he dropped his head back to the mattress. "I love you, Tor."

My body went rigid.

His didn't, though.

His hand just moved lightly over my back as he added, "You're not obligated to feel the same. I know it'll take you longer to fall for me, but I need you to know that I do. I love you."

I closed my eyes, and let out a slow breath.

I... wasn't sure how I felt.

On one hand, there was a lot between us we still needed to figure out. The day-to-day life thing was still an unknown.

But there was no denying that I felt connected to him. That I couldn't walk away from him, and that I didn't *want* to.

Maybe I wasn't sure I was in love with him, but there was no way around the fact that I wanted to get there.

So I whispered, "I'm not ready to say I love you... but I'm yours."

Ronin's body went rigid.

His hand pressed down lightly on my back, pushing me closer to him. Tighter to him.

"Tori," he said, his voice low.

Hopeful.

But uncertain, too.

The hope I'd heard in it propelled me. "I've been yours for a while, even if I wasn't ready to admit it," I said. "Love will take time, but... I think I'm ready to commit. I don't want out anymore. I want you. I want to be your mate."

"You have me. You've always had me." He tilted my face up and kissed me. The kiss was gentle at first, but grew hotter fast.

When he pulled away, I was breathing quickly.

"*Aeternum*, Tor." His words were low, smooth, and sure. Even if I hadn't known the meaning behind them, I still would've felt the intense, ancient magic of them.

*Aeternum* was the word that could create a mate bond, if both parties agreed.

Ronin didn't have a shred of doubt about us.

And while there were still a million things I wasn't sure about, there was one thing I knew:

I was never going to walk away from him.

So I swallowed my fear of commitment and said, "*Aeternum*, Alpha."

The magic that would bind us rolled over me and through me.

It tingled.

It warmed me.

It even burned a little.

But it was perfect. All of it was.

Ronin's lips captured mine again, the kiss slow and intimate.

He pulled me further up his body as our tongue's warred—and only released me long enough to let me gasp when he slid inside me again.

We moved as one, and it didn't feel like fucking anymore.

It felt like making love.

Like the start of something so much bigger than either of us.

And honestly, I couldn't wait to see where it carried us.

## epilogue

### RONIN

AFTER TWO WEEKS went by without another sign of a vampire, Tori finally convinced me to take her home.

I didn't put up much of a fight.

She wasn't the only one tired of the constant knowing looks, winks, and congratulations of the Wildwood pack.

She met my pack's members throughout the week. By the time we got back to our own chunk of land, she had already joined the ranks as officially as we did anything.

We didn't have pack meetings, or gathered events. We were just a family.

I didn't like knowing my female was the only woman in the pack, but I wanted her with me, so there was no way around that.

And besides, she was mine.

Permanently.

She'd declared so herself.

We had an unofficial barbecue the night we got back to our houses, just to kick off having her there. Tori chatted with everyone while she sat at my side, my fingers linked with hers. She brought life to our group in a way I hadn't dared hope for—and I loved that intensely.

After we all ate ourselves sick, we shifted, and let our wolves run free. Tori's wolf ran beside mine, teasing him and playing with him. They brought each other out of their shells, and I fucking loved it.

When we finally made it back home in the middle of the night, we collapsed in bed without bothering to shower. Tori snuggled her bare body up against mine, and I held her tight.

I'd just been existing, before I found her.

Now that I had her, I was finally alive.

"You're a good mate," she mumbled to me. "The best, actually."

My chest and throat burned with emotion.

The woman couldn't have given me a better compliment, no matter how hard she tried.

She peeked up at me through her long lashes, a smile on her face. "You're still terrible at taking compliments, you know. The way you blush is adorable."

"I'm an alpha, woman. There's nothing adorable about me," I grumbled, though I didn't feel the offense I was feigning. Not even a little.

She laughed. "Whatever you say."

When she tilted her face back, I kissed her deeply.

Passionately.

With everything I had.

"Maybe I do love you," she murmured.

"I'm going to need more certainty than that, Tor."

She laughed again, harder. "Fuck, you're cute. I'm glad we're stuck together."

"Me too." I squeezed her lightly. "Now go to sleep."

"Yes, Alpha," she teased.

I pulled her closer, and couldn't help but watch as she dozed off in my arms.

In *our* bed.

In *our* home.

Life was fucking perfect.

# afterthoughts

I don't read books without happy endings.
If you've read many of my books—or even just this one—
that probably won't come as a surprise to you.
I read to escape.
To live in another person's world for a few hours.
I like books that make me smile, laugh, and feel good.
Considering you made it this far, I hope you do too!
Anyway, I love that not all books have to be long and
dramatic. I love that they can be short, fun, and sweet. And
while I don't know what I'll want to write next month, or
next year, I'm having a ton of fun with these easy, happy
romances.
I can't wait to see Sienna and Bauther's story unfold!
Something tells me it's going to be a spicy one, so get your
fans ready ;)
All the love,
Lola Glass <3

# *stay in touch*

Stay in Touch

If you want to receive Lola's newsletter for new releases (no spam!) use this link:

LINK

Or find her on:
FACEBOOK
TIKTOK
INSTAGRAM

PINTEREST

GOODREADS

Many of the standalones

# *all series by lola glass*

**Check out Lola's website for a guide to which of her series are connected!**

https://www.authorlolaglass.com/where-do-i-start

### *Standalones:*

Wildwood

Deceit & Devotion

Claimed by the Wolf

Forbidden Mates

Wild Hunt

Kings of Disaster

Night's Curse

Outcast Pack

Feral Pack

Mate Hunt

### *Series:*

Burning Kingdom

Sacrificed to the Fae King

Shifter Queen

Wolfsbane

Shifter City

Supernatural Underworld

Moon of the Monsters

Rejected Mate Refuge

## about the author

Lola is a book-lover with a *slight* romance obsession and a passion for love—real love. Not the flowers-and-chocolates kind of love, but the kind where two people build a relationship strong enough to last. That's the kind of relationship she loves to read about, and the kind she tries to portray in her books.

Even though they're fun stories about sassy women and huge, growly magical men ;)